Grace

Space

A Direct Sales Tale

ROBIN MERRILL

New Creation Publishing

GRACE SPACE: A DIRECT SALES TALE

Copyright © 2014 by Robin Merrill

Published by New Creation Publishing

Scripture quotation taken from the New American Standard Bible®, Copyright © 1960, 1962, 1963, 1968, 1971, 1972, 1973, 1975, 1977, 1995 by The Lockman Foundation. Used by permission. (www.Lockman.org)

Cover Design: Taste & See Design
Formatting by Perry Elisabeth Design | perryelisabethdesign.com

ISBN-10: 0991270649
ISBN-13: 978-0-9912706-4-4

For my ever patient husband.

Prologue

Please understand. I was only in it for the money. Looking back, I recognize the many ways I could have done things differently. I could've made better choices. This is an embarrassing tale to tell. But I want to be honest. Perhaps my mistakes will help you avoid similar mistakes of your own. Or perhaps my mistakes will help you tip your head back, whoop with laughter, and slap your leg till it hurts. If I had to choose a single goal for this letter, it would be the latter.

Chapter 1
In the Beginning …

While I am fairly ashamed of many of my decisions, the outcome of this story leaves no room for regrets. So stick with me. I do come out of all this in pretty good shape.

I was a proud English teacher. I was a proud, unemployed English teacher. Two years out of teaching college, whence I proudly graduated with a 3.7, I landed a job as an ed tech, but then my student moved away and I was back to serving tables. I wasn't all that torn up. The week before he moved away, that student tried to staple my hand to the desk.

Back to my childhood bedroom I went. I was twenty-four and sleeping in a bunk bed. (I slept on the top bunk to avoid competing with my parents' three Labrador retrievers for real estate.)

I had a monthly student loan payment of five hundred dollars. I was desperate. I was also bored. Not a good combination. So when Tally, my fellow table server, invited me to a "Grace Space Celebration," I cheerfully accepted. It was either that or reruns of *Bonanza* with my dad.

I arrived to Tally's apartment with bells on and found a large platter of cheese and crackers. As I loaded up with Triscuits and sharp cheddar, a perfectly accessorized, smiling woman introduced herself as Lisa. She shook my hand and told me she was a "Grace Space Independent Consultant." She seemed innocuous enough, though her Easter-egg-purple-skirt-suit seemed a bit much for the occasion.

Lisa asked us to gather around her display, and a substantial display it was. I had never seen so many products in one place. Truth be told, I didn't know there were so many products in the world. I counted six distinct eye creams. I tried to think of six different eye problems in need of treatment, but I couldn't.

But I'm not really a product kind of girl. I'm a deodorant (usually) and mascara (on weekends) kind of girl. So I sort of zoned out during Lisa's well-communicated presentation. Something about fine lines and wrinkles and slimming earrings—I don't know—but the second she said "forty dollars an hour," I transformed into a homing missile, completely focused on my target.

"*Forty what?*" I interrupted.

She didn't seem to mind. "Yes, it's true," she said, "the average Grace Space Independent Consultant earns forty dollars per hour."

Now, *that* impressed me. I was working for FOUR dollars an hour, plus tips of course, but sometimes those tips never showed up. Sometimes I got phone numbers instead of tips. It's hard to make student loan payments with unsolicited phone numbers. And, if I am completely transparent, Lisa impressed me too. There was just something about her. I suppose it was charisma. She was like the cool girl in high school you just wanted to hang out with. She was pretty, charming, and confident. I just wanted to be her friend. I wanted her to like me.

At the end of her demonstration, she took each of us into another room, one at a time. Something about privacy and money transactions. I didn't want to buy anything, but I did want Lisa to like me, so I spent twenty-four of my hard-earned dollars on a lip revival kit. I figured I'd stack up on cheddar on my way out to make up for it. Then she asked me: "Darcy, would you do me a big favor?"

I could hardly contain my excitement. Of course I would do her a favor.

"Would you be a model for me next Monday night? I have to go to this makeup training and I think you would make a great model. You have such high cheekbones."

Sold.

No one had ever said anything nice about my cheekbones before. No one had ever said anything about my cheekbones period.

And that's how I ended up at a Grace Space family meeting the following Monday.

Since that night, I've been to countless Grace Space family meetings and they have all sort of melded together in my mind into one tragic lump, but I'll try to recall the high points of that first experience for you.

First, you need to know about Priscilla.

Priscilla introduced herself to me as a Grace Space Independent Regional Sales and Marketing Manager. I tried to quip about Grace coming up with some shorter job titles, and Priscilla looked like I'd shoved some sour candy in her mouth. But she seemed nice enough. She was wearing a purple skirt suit too, but this was a different shade of purple, a darker purple. I would learn to identify this specific shade as sinister, but back then I just thought it was *really* purple.

In fact, in Grace Space lingo, Priscilla *was* a purple.

I learned that night that my new friend Lisa was only a lilac.

There were dozens of other women milling about in lilac suits. And there were just a few sporting a medium shade. Those were the violets.

Are you confused yet? I certainly was. It felt as if I were drowning in a purple ocean of perfume and hair spray.

But Lisa stayed right by my side, making me feel like one of the cool kids. I learned that we were, in fact, in Priscilla's home that night—in the Grace Space *wing*: a giant open room with a small kitchenette and bar tucked into one corner and copious amounts of folding chairs.

Lisa guided me to a corner of the oddly large room, opened her tackle box of product and paraphernalia, and set to work on my cheekbones. I won't lie—I loved having Lisa's undivided attention. She was just so *nice* to me. If you've ever waited tables, you know that a girl can go many days in a row without anyone being nice to her.

I wasn't the only "model" there. There were three of us. But I went first. I was instructed to walk, slowly, down an intimidating narrow aisle between the folding chairs while Lisa talked about what she had done to my face. I couldn't hear what she was saying about me because I was focusing on putting one awkward foot in front of the other with all of these purple people staring at me. The room was remarkably dimly lit, which is always a good thing in my book, so I wondered how they could even see my makeup, but they certainly seemed to be trying. All of them. Staring at me. All of them. Smiling. All of them. Heavily lipsticked smiles.

I was so grateful to sit down.

Then Priscilla got up to "teach." She talked about taxes. It was August. I briefly wondered why they were worried about taxes in August, but I was quickly distracted by the figures she was throwing out. She talked about all the write-offs—in fact, the very wing we inhabited? Monster write-off! She talked about how big her tax return always is and she made a joke about not giving any of her hard-earned cash to the government. This got a hearty laugh from the purple peanut gallery. But I never heard a single word past this phrase: *I made more than 300,000 dollars last year.*

What?! Excuse me? There is no way I heard that correctly. But that *is* what she said. Three hundred thousand buckaroos. Un*real*.

So, in the dark car on the way home, when Lisa said, "Would you ever consider working with me?" I did not hesitate. When she took me to her apartment instead of my parents' house, I signed on the dotted line. When she asked me for three hundred dollars for my kickoff kit, I handed her the MasterCard.

Let the games begin.

Chapter 2
A Lilac Is Born

No one mentioned God at that first Grace Space family meeting.

They mentioned him at the next one. In fact, Priscilla opened with prayer. I soon learned that there were "open family meetings" and "closed family meetings." Of course, I had been to the former the first time. They don't pray at those.

I drove myself to my first closed family meeting. Priscilla's Grace Space castle was in Waterville, Maine, just across the river from my hometown. I was greeted at the door by a lilac I didn't know. She hugged me.

She smelled strongly of Camels (the cigarettes, not the humped animals). I later learned that Priscilla posted a lilac at the door of closed meetings to make sure no one brought friends. The day would come when I would take my turn at standing guard. Officially, I would be called a Grace Greeter.

I weaved my way through shades of purple and then Priscilla found me. She hugged me. "Have you hugged your mother yet?"

"Excuse me?" I wasn't trying to be sassy. I just didn't know my mother had been invited to the meeting.

But Priscilla had little patience for my confusion. She made the sour candy face again. "Lisa. Your recruiter. Grace Space is a family. She's your Grace Space mother."

"Uh ... oh. Sorry. No, I haven't seen her."

"Well, find her. And sit with her. She has lots to teach you. Have you met your grandmother?"

I couldn't help it. I snickered. The candy in her mouth got even sourer. "Uh ... are you my grandmother?"

She sighed as if she were talking to a stupid child. In a way, I guess she was. "No. I am your *great* grandmother. Dominique is your grandmother. She's a violet."

"Ah, I see," I said, though I didn't really see at all. I ran away and desperately searched for Lisa.

I found her sitting in the front row. She jumped up and hugged me. I sat down beside her. She handed me a thick folder. It was purple.

"Here is some stuff you'll need. Product order forms. Recruitment forms. Some motivational literature … oh, and you'll want to order your suit, pronto," she said flipping open the folder to a suit order form. I groaned a little. Then I groaned a lot when I saw the suit cost ninety-five dollars.

"Seriously? I don't have ninety-five dollars! Shouldn't the suit come with the kickoff kit? I didn't know I would have to buy my own suit?"

"Shh," Lisa held a finger up to her lips. "There are other new lilacs here, and we don't want to plant negative seeds," she whispered.

I looked around furtively, but I was the only one in the room not wearing purple.

"Oh, uh, sorry. Well, can I wait till I make some money at this before I order my suit?"

"No," Lisa whispered, "because you aren't allowed to do any celebrations without your suit."

Of course I wasn't. It hit me, only then, that I would have to start wearing skirts. And panty hose. And non-canvas shoes.

"Lisa?" I whispered. (The whispering was contagious.) She raised her eyebrows. "How many lilac suits do you own?"

She smiled. "Only two. I don't plan to be a lilac for long."

Priscilla called the meeting to order and asked us to bow our heads and close our eyes.

"Father in Heaven," she began, "we thank you for your grace. We thank you for bringing us here together tonight. Please help us to serve you and to serve others. We ask you to bless us financially as we work to honor you. Amen."

To be honest, I hadn't prayed in a while, but something about that prayer annoyed me. I wasn't quite sure what, and didn't have time to figure it out, because Priscilla was telling us to take notes. Oh no! I hadn't even brought a pen. I looked down at my purple folder in order to avoid her sour candy gaze.

She talked about recruiting. She said things like, "You need to make women feel special," and "Make them want to be your friend." I stole a glance at Lisa. She was staring at Priscilla like she was looking at a prophet.

A small voice in my head said something along the lines of, *You've been manipulated, and they're not even trying to hide it. Lisa doesn't like you! She was just following her training.* I tried to push that voice down in the name of 300,000 dollars per year.

The meeting was long. I found myself planning to bring a butt pillow to the next family meeting. I found myself wondering how Priscilla had ever become the manager of *this many* women. She was the only purple suit in the room, so I assumed she was in charge. We were also in her house, or at least a wing of it.

Lisa walked me out and asked me if I wanted to get coffee the next morning. Her invitation offered me much solace, but, alas, I told her I had to work.

"When are you going to quit your waitress job?"

I belted out a laugh. "What?"

"Well, now that you're in Grace Space, you don't need to be a *waitress*." She pronounced waitress like it was a really dirty thing.

I laughed again, because I was uncomfortable, not because anything was funny. "First of all, we prefer the term *server*. Second of all, I probably shouldn't quit until I actually *make some money*. I mean, I can't even afford a suit."

"Okay," she said, making a toss-the-hair-over-her-shoulder move, even though none of her hair actually moved, "you're in charge of your own career." I detected a smidge of condescension. "Just know that a waitressing job will eat up a lot of your time and won't help advance your career. You could be spending this time training and studying and getting to know the product. But, you can choose what you want to be."

I opened my mouth to defend myself, but before I could, she added, "Let me know when you want to get coffee and we can go over your folder. In the meantime, be sure you go over the checklist. Good night!" And with that, Lisa hugged me again and then disappeared into the night, leaving me beside my car wondering why these women hug so much. I mean, this is New England for crying out loud.

When I got home, I went to the Grace Space website and used my MasterCard to order a lilac suit.

Chapter 3
The Checklist

It wasn't until the following evening that I got to the checklist. Most of the material in my folder was company produced. Glossy, professional-looking pamphlets full of shiny products and equally shiny women.

The checklist didn't look like this.

The checklist looked like something that had been typed up thirty years ago and then mimeographed in my kindergarten classroom. These were the days before spellcheck. These were not the days before caps lock.

THE CHECKLIST

Welcome to Grace Space! Here is a list of things that you can do to get your Grace Space career off and ruining! These are not orders, these are simple suggestions from your grandmothers, the women who have been doing this successfuly for a while now! We know what works!

1. THROW AWAY (throw-don't give) all your old makeup and jewelry. From now on, it's GRACE SPACE OR NOTHING!

2. Join a church. If your church already has a Grace Space consultant, join a different church.

3. Join a book club. You usually don't' have to read the books. You just have to show up and hang out. Plus, you can RECOMMEND GRACE SPACE BOOKS!!!

4. From now on, never ever ever ever leave the house without LOOKING YOUR BEST. Practice on yourself ALOT! Get used to looking GREAT

5. Call your mother at least once a day, just to check in. Call your grandmother weekly. Only call your great-grandmohter in emergencies.

6. Join an aerobics class. You need to be fit and this is a great place to RECRUIT MORE GRACIES.

7. Find childcare. We love children and we love children because we love children, we want to give them the best life possible. So you need to

find regular childcare so that you can invest yourelf in Grace Space.

Okay, so I know. I should have quit right then and there. The English teacher within me almost died at the sight of so many errors in one place. And, what the heck is a gracie? But I had already ordered the kickoff kit. And I had already ordered a lilac suit. And I really hated serving tables. And I really wanted to make 300,000 dollars a year. And I really wanted to make last month's student loan payment. And I had to be at least as smart as Priscilla, right? If she could do it, so could I, right?

All I had to get rid of was an old tube of solidified mascara and a class ring. I threw away one and decided I could probably get away with keeping the other. There, that was easy. Now, for the next checkmark.

Joining a church.

I grew up in the church, but I had totally gotten out of the church habit when I went to college. While I had absolutely no idea why my church attendance might matter to Grace Space, I did recognize that going to church would be a good idea. I vowed to go to church on Sunday.

At that point, my mother walked into her living room. I shoved the checklist in between the couch cushions. As I pulled my hand back out, a Cheeto popped out. I considered eating it. I was hungry. I tossed it to Lab Number Two instead.

I had already told my parents about my grand Grace Space plans, but they were less than supportive. Dad called me "foolish" and Mom told me that Grace Space was a "nothin' but a makeup cult."

"Yes, but Priscilla makes 300,000 dollars a year!" I had argued.

And Mom had retorted in the most condescending voice possible, "Honey, if something is too good to be true, it is."

"So you're saying that Priscilla is lying?" I challenged.

Mom didn't answer this, just obnoxiously rolled her eyes at Dad, who said, "Don't invest any actual money in this harebrained scheme. It's a con."

There was a bunch of eye-rolling on Sunday morning when I left the house before the church bells rang. My family had gone to a nearby church when I was a kid, but my parents had fallen out of the habit as much as I had. Still, I defaulted to that same church. Besides, it was only a block away.

The sign outside said: "All are welcome!" This made me feel welcome. A few people greeted me with handshakes and smiles. No one seemed to remember me. This was okay. The choir sang a few songs and then the pastor, who was shorter than I remembered, delivered a sermon that was also shorter than the ones I remembered.

His message focused on how we are supposed to do everything as if we are doing it for Jesus. Absurdly, I imagined applying Jesus' eyeliner, and had to choke down a laugh. Still, it felt good to be back in the pews, and I left there with a genuine feeling of peace in my heart. Maybe this Grace Space gig wouldn't be so bad after all.

I got a call from Priscilla that afternoon.

"Hello?"

"Good afternoon, this is Priscilla Green."

I could almost hear the sour candy.

"Hi, Priscilla, what's up?"

"Suzanne Frazer says she saw you in church this morning."

"Oh, yes," I said, "I went to a really great church near my—"

"Well, that's *Suzanne's church*," Priscilla interrupted.

I felt a little like crying. I wasn't the type of girl who got scolded. I paused, tried to collect myself. "Oh … sorry … I didn't know."

"That's okay, Darcy. That's what we figured. Just try to find a church that doesn't already have a Grace Space presence."

At that point, you might think I would just give up on that particular checkmark, but I had really enjoyed church that morning. I *wanted* to go back to that church and was annoyed that I couldn't. I figured the next best thing was to find a church I *could* go to. "Do you know of a church that's available?" I asked with no little attitude in my voice.

"The only one I know of at the moment is New Life Church. It's on 201, between Fairfield and

Skowhegan. It's small, but I'm pretty sure it's available."

"Okay, thanks," I said because I didn't know what else to say.

"You're welcome," she answered as if I had meant my thanks.

Chapter 4
Showtime

I came home from my lowly waitressing job the next afternoon to find four boxes—three giant and one small—propped against the base of my parents' mailbox. The boxes were emblazoned with Grace Space logos and I paused momentarily to be embarrassed.

As I lugged the boxes up the steps against a tide of Labradors, I noticed my parents' neighbor watching me. Steven (not Steve, I had learned long ago, but Steven) had grown up in the house across the street and still lived there. But! My mother made sure I knew, Steven didn't live *with* his parents—he had bought the house from them and they had retired to Florida. Mom also told me that Steven was a *successful* photographer with many *successful* shows and many *successful* publications. Despite how many times Mom used the word successful, Steven still gave me the creeps. I was pretty sure I had caught him taking my picture from across the street, or at least looking at me through a telephoto lens.

"I see you're taking up Grace Space," Steven hollered across the street. "That doesn't really seem like you."

"Yep," I said, trying to shut the conversation down before it started, and wondering how he knew what was and wasn't me.

"Who's your team leader?" he asked.

Honestly baffled, I said, "Huh?"

He smiled. "Your recruiter. Who is making money off you?"

I really didn't want to answer him, but I had no idea what else to say, so I said, "Lisa Provost."

"Oh, never heard of her," he said, as if that was a real shocker. I flashed him a fake smile and let the screen door bang behind me.

I'll be honest—it was pretty fun ripping into those boxes. There were so many pretty things inside! I didn't know what a lot of them were, but they were so shiny! Display stands, jewelry, makeup and perfume samples, cotton balls, and mirrors. Boxes and boxes. I started to honestly think this might be fun. It would certainly be more fun than bussing tables and scrubbing high chairs.

The smaller box held the requisite lilac skirt suit. Good grief was it ugly! The fabric was itchy and thick. I groaned at the dry clean only tag. I wondered why any marketing guru would make her salespeople wear hot, thick, dry clean only suits in August.

At the family meeting that night, as if on cue, Lisa asked, "Did you get your kickoff kit yet?"

"Yep," I said with excitement I didn't even have to fake. I was finally ready to make some of that money I'd been hearing so much about.

"Great, 'cause I have a celebration you can have if you want."

"Seriously?" I was shocked. Why would Lisa give up one of her money-making opportunities?

"Yep, I double booked myself for this Saturday, so you would be doing me a big favor if you took one of the celebrations."

I wondered why she would double book herself (later I would learn this was S.O.P.), but I gratefully agreed to help her out. "I don't think I'm ready, though. Isn't there more I should know? Shouldn't I be trained or something?" I asked.

She paused, "No, you're all set. You watched me do a celebration. You've been to a few family meetings. You've got a stack of catalogs and some samples. You should be all set."

"But I want to know what I'm doing. I just figured there would be more instruction or something." A small but mighty panic was setting in.

"Nope. You'll be fine. Just relax and have fun." She handed me a scrap of paper with an address written on it and told me to get there an hour early, at one o'clock sharp.

"Oh no!" I said. "I don't get out of work until two. I guess I can't do this after all. I just assumed that she would have her party at night."

"It's a celebration, not a party."

"Uh, okay, not really sure what the difference is."

"The word 'party' puts too much pressure on a hostess. Anyway, you need to call in or switch shifts with someone. Don't let a waitressing job mess up your future."

I laughed a little. I couldn't help it. "Lisa, I'm not sure this is my future. I'm just doing this to make a little bit of money."

She was silent for a moment, and my stomach sank at the thought that I had offended my cool new friend. "Well, Darcy, that's up to you. We all make our own decisions. Do you want the celebration or not?"

All I could think about was undoing the damage that I had just done to this new friendship. I didn't think about my boss or coworkers at the restaurant. I just thought about what Lisa thought about me. "Yeah, I'll take it. I'll figure something out."

"Great. Good luck." And she was gone, absorbed back into the purple sea.

The next morning, I asked for Saturday off.

"Absolutely not."

I was instantly embarrassed. Of course the answer was no. What did I expect? So I asked Tally to switch shifts with me. "I don't really want to give up any of my shifts," she said, "but I'll just take that one for you if you want. I could use the extra cash." I quickly agreed. That was perfect. I would lose out on about fifty bucks, but I assumed I would make more than that at my first celebration.

Turns out I was a *little* off on that assumption.

I arrived to my first celebration right on time. My hostess's name was Marty. Marty lived in a duplex that had seen better days. I didn't mean to be judgmental— I was pretty broke myself. But when I parked my car in that neighborhood, I was glad that my car wasn't worth stealing.

I was super nervous, but Marty was nice enough and she put me right at ease. The inside of her home was neat as a pin, and I instantly felt bad for judging the outside. She explained to me that she knew Lisa from church. I took my time setting up my display, and when I was done, I felt like an idiot.

I had it in my head that my display would automatically look as awesome as Lisa's had. But once I was set up, I realized that Lisa was working with way more than a kickoff kit. Spread out on Marty's bar, my "display" looked like the top of a well-organized preteen's dresser. I fanned out the catalogs so that they would take up more space and I took a deep breath.

All told, it took me five minutes to set up, and that included a trip to the bathroom, so I'm not sure why Grace Space dictates the hour early rule, but Marty and I chatted the hour away. I knew that I was supposed to be recruiting her to sell Grace Space too, but that just felt wrong, especially since I hadn't sold so much as an earring yet.

It wasn't long before the guests starting rolling in—both of them. The four of us sat around Marty's kitchen table and I grudgingly read the intro from my training manual:

Grace Space was started in 1992 by a group of Christian moms who wanted to help support their families. Today, those women are millionaires. By God's grace, Grace Space took off and grew like wildfire. Grace Space helps women to bring out their inner beauty through a high quality line of affordable beauty products and accessories. We also continue to offer women a flexible way to earn an income. So welcome to Grace Space. Now the question is, *how can we make you feel beautiful today?*

I felt like someone else when I was speaking the lines.

Chapter 5
All My Fault

I was mad. Today, that anger seems silly. Considering what *can* go wrong at a Grace Space "celebration," that first party wasn't so bad. But it felt bad at the time.

I sold one lip balm for eight dollars. I sold one necklace for thirteen. I sold a grand total of twenty-one dollars' worth of Grace Space paraphernalia. That night, I earned a whopping seven bucks. I had spent four dollars in gas to get to the party and back. And I had gone through quite a few of the makeup samples that came as part of the kickoff kit.

When I mistakenly mentioned this math to Lisa over the phone, it quickly became my fault. "Well," she snapped, as if I were an incredibly stupid child, "Did you do their whole face?"

"Huh?"

"Did you give them enough makeup samples for their whole face?"

"Uh, yeah. Yes I did."

"Well, that was your mistake. You only do half their faces. That way they can see how much better they look with Grace Space on their face."

I couldn't help it. I laughed out loud at "Grace Space on their face." The phrase conjured up images of pasting the actual catalog to the women's faces.

"So," I began to reason, "I expect them to happily leave the party with makeup on only half their faces? Won't this make them look ridiculous? Don't women get annoyed? And how was I supposed to know that I was only supposed to do half their faces? No one ever told me that!"

Lisa heaved a theatrical sigh. "Look, if you have a problem with this, then just do the makeup on the hostess. Then this will motivate all the guests to book their own celebrations, so that they can then sample the makeup. You *did* book other celebrations off this celebration, didn't you?"

The word celebration was starting to give me a headache. "Uh, Lisa? There were only two people there. And no, they didn't book parties. The whole thing was a lame flop. Why would they want to create such a thing in their own homes?"

"A lame flop? Darcy, your success is up to you! You can't allow a celebration to become a lame flop, and if you don't book a celebration off a celebration, then you are dead in the water! Now you have nothing on your calendar and you're going to have to start from scratch!"

For just a moment, I stopped caring about how cool Lisa was. I came back to myself long enough to say, "Lisa, maybe I'm not cut out for this."

And in less than a second, Lisa transformed from scary-shrieky-lilac-mode to sweet-soothing-life-coach-mode. "Oh Darcy, I went through all this too. It's hard getting started, but you can do it. I know you can do it. Don't worry, hon, I'll find you another booking."

"Thanks, Lisa," I said, "I'm just a bit concerned because I've invested 395 dollars in this thing so far. And I barely broke even at my first celebration. And I gave up a shift at work for this, so really, I'm even deeper in the hole."

"No sweetie, you're not in a hole at all. You are just invested. We all need to be invested. You got professional sales experience last night, and that is priceless. You made connections with women, connections that no one can take away from you. You are building a bright and beautiful foundation. Don't you worry! You're going to be great! It takes a lot of hard work to reach your goals, but you can do it! I know you can!"

"Thanks, Lisa. I appreciate that."

"Oh, you're very welcome. I recommend calling those celebration guests and following up. Offer them some incentive to book a celebration with you."

"Oh" I said without thinking, "but I didn't get their phone numbers."

"*What?*" Lisa said, and it was obvious she was struggling to control her emotions. "Darcy, how could you not get their phone numbers?"

I gave up. "Lisa, I have to go now. I'm sick of this. I told you I didn't have enough training to do all this. No one told me to get phone numbers. No one told me how to book parties from parties. No one told me that I'm supposed to only do half their faces. I have to go. Talk to you later." And I hung up.

I should have counted. I didn't, but I think I can accurately estimate that it was sixty seconds before my phone rang.

"Hello?" I said.

"Hello, darling, this is your grandmother calling."

Chapter 6
The Smell of Money

I hadn't actually met Dominique yet, so I couldn't picture the face that was currently speaking. But she certainly sounded as if she knew me. Her voice was so empathic, so soothing, so ... *convincing*. Her spoken lullaby convinced me again that Grace Space was for me and that together, we could make all my dreams come true.

She asked me if I had "run out of" friends and family yet. I didn't know what she meant. She clarified: Had I tried to book celebrations with friends and relatives yet?

I explained, "I'm kind of an introvert. I don't really have any friends."

She clarified again, "I'm talking about third cousins and old high school friends, anyone you know or have ever known."

I was a bit mortified, but Dominique made it up to me by also offering me one of her already booked celebrations.

So that is how, that very night, I ended up driving seventy miles to a beautiful house in Falmouth. Quite a different scene from my first celebration. I got lost weaving up and down peninsulas so I skated into Julie's house just barely on time. It was raining out, and her house was so fancy, I felt shame for dripping water on her pristine floor.

Her guests were already there. Eight ladies who looked about retirement age stood around a table full of snacks. There was actually a punch bowl. They were all dressed in clothes nicer than anything I'd ever worn. They had good hair, lots of jewelry, and makeup. I could practically smell their money. At the time, this didn't alarm me, but looking back, I am a little spooked by how quickly I went from "never think about money" to "guessing women's socioeconomic status at a glance."

Financially, that party was a roaring success. The women were rude and condescending, but they had credit cards. And they seemed to be in a contest to see who could spend more. I obligatorily took each of them into a separate room to do their orders, and several of them asked me what others had bought.

According the Grace Space etiquette, the whole point of taking women into a separate room to order is to keep financial matters private. I later learned that the real motivation lies in the idea that it's easier to manipulate and pressure women when you get them one on one. Either way, that evening, I was happy to share privileged information with whoever asked: "Yes, Patricia, Ruth spent over two hundred dollars!"

When I asked Patricia if she wanted to host a celebration of her own, she said she would love to, but that she lived in Lowell, Massachusetts. I, without thinking much about my tired car, said that wouldn't be a problem. And so, Darcy had finally booked her very own celebration. I was so proud.

No really. I was.

I was so proud that I woke up the next morning and started contacting my cousins. I crafted a compelling generic Facebook message and sent it to every female I was "friends" with. I told them about my new Grace Space adventure, lied and said I was having a lot of fun, and offered a free mascara to anyone who placed an order or booked a celebration with me.

Sounds pretty smart, right? I thought it was. I was rather proud of myself. But no one responded. No one.

I shared this disappointment with Lisa, who told me, "Grace Space doesn't work that way. You have to call."

So, a few days later, with a giant knot in my gut, I called Anna, my nicest cousin. I hadn't seen her in years, but we had gotten along fabulously when we were kids.

"Hello?"

"Hi, Anna! This is Darcy!" I said, trying futilely to sound both peppy and natural. "How are you?"

I could hear it in her voice. She knew why I was calling, and she was sorry she had answered the phone.

"Hi, Darcy, I'm great. You?"

"I'm fantastic," I lied. "I'm just calling to follow up on the Facebook message I sent. Did you get it?"

"Yes, I did Darcy, but I'm just not interested. Sorry."

"No problem," I lied. "Just let me know if you change your mind."

"I will, Darcy. You take care, and good luck." And she was gone.

I sat there holding the phone, wondering what had gone wrong. Surely this isn't the way it worked for Dominique and Lisa? Otherwise, they wouldn't have encouraged me to do this. I figured that Anna must have just been a fluke. Truth be told, she wasn't really the Grace Space type. She was an outdoorsy, all natural sort of girl. I should have thought of that.

I scanned my brain for a contact who was a bit more high maintenance. And I remembered my high school friend Genevieve. Of course! This time, I wrote down a script, including what I would say in response to any "no" that Genevieve could throw at me.

I was much more prepared when I dialed Genevieve's phone number, and the pit in my stomach had shrunk.

But her number was disconnected. Of course it was. I hadn't called her in years. Why would her number be the same? I sent her a Facebook message, "Hey Genna, I just tried to call you, but your number has changed. Would love to reconnect. What's your new number?"

I wasn't surprised when she didn't answer. I was surprised later that day to find she had blocked me on Facebook. Now *that* was embarrassing. No one had ever blocked me from anything. How rude!

Thinking about Genevieve made me think of her friend Marina. Marina's Facebook was linked to her cell, so I called her up, prepared to use the same script I had drafted for Genevieve, but when Marina said, "Oh hey, Darcy. Good to hear from you, but I actually used to be a Grace Space consultant, and well, it didn't end well for me." I had no idea what to say. I hadn't drafted a response for that yet.

So I said, "I'm sorry to hear that Marina. What happened?"

"You'll find out. Good luck."

Huh. That was ominous. But I was undeterred.

I racked my brain and came up with some more ways that people could say "no" to me and then I drafted some more ways to respond. I remember thinking *this* would have been useful information for the welcome packet and vowed to share my growing phone script with my future recruits.

I decided to call Alexis. We had played soccer together. She still lived in town. As soon as I said the words "Grace Space," Alexis hung up on me. No excuse. Just a cold click. This hurt my feelings. I sat there in shock, tears sliding down my face. I was deterred. So I did what any wounded fledgling would do. I called my mother.

"Hello?"

"Lisa! Dominique told me to call my friends and family, but it's not working. Someone just hung up on me! Are people always this mean?"

"Oh Darcy," Lisa said soothingly, "you can't take it personally."

"What?" I asked. "How can I not take it personally? She hung up on *me! Me personally! That's pretty personal!*" I was whining. I couldn't help it.

"No, she didn't hang up on you, she hung up on Grace Space. Don't be sad for you. Be sad for her. She's missing out on the opportunity of a lifetime. But you just have to move on. You'll forget all about it when your next phone call results in a connection. You've just got to keep keeping on! The next phone call could be the one that launches your career!"

This wasn't helping.

I wrapped up my conversation with Lisa and returned to my list. And I called everyone. I mean *everyone* I knew. No one launched my career into anything. Another old soccer teammate told me, "I think the market is pretty saturated. You should try to sell something that everyone else isn't already selling."

My old college roommate said, "That stuff makes me break out."

My aunt Mary: "Didn't you go to college?"

My cousin Jen: "Sorry, I sell Arbonne. It's all natural. And vegan."

My old biology lab partner: "Grace Space is a pyramid scheme."

And my personal favorite, from the teacher who had supervised my practicum: "I want nothing to do with a company that aligns itself with bigoted fundamentalism."

I would have smashed the phone, but I couldn't afford to buy my parents a new phone. So I went and lay down on the couch. I stared at the ceiling, thanking God that my parents weren't home to ask me what was wrong.

Chapter 7
New Life

New Life Church was new indeed. Actually, the building looked kind of ancient, but everything about the church was new to me.

First of all, the church was *tiny*. There were about thirty people there, so it was impossible to go unnoticed. Second of all, this church was *the friendliest church in the universe*. I'm pretty sure every single person struck up a conversation with me, and they seemed genuinely interested in my life—even the kids. A girl of about seven told me she liked my shoes. This pleased me. I had just bought them for Grace Space events and my feet were *killing* me. But hey, I had impressed a seven-year-old. I remember feeling oddly, I don't know, *settled* at New Life, like I belonged there, maybe even like I had always belonged there.

The service officially began when an (unbelievably gorgeous) man began to pound on the drums. In a few measures, an electric guitar and a bass joined in, and then the lead singer began to belt out a song I'd never heard before. The people around me began to clap and dance and throw their hands up in the air, and I wondered what planet I was on. Truth be told, I was a little freaked out, but that "belonging" feeling never left me. I remember thinking that if Pricilla told me I couldn't go to this church, I would most certainly disobey her.

After the service, the congregation gathered in the basement for brunch. Considering the attendance, the spread was impressive, and I got to talk to the drummer. It's a good thing the sermon had been about lust, because this man was *that* attractive. His name was Luke. He was a construction foreman in Waterville. He was friendly. He wasn't wearing a wedding ring. When he asked me what I did for a living, I told him I worked at Kassandra's Diner on Garfield Street. He nodded knowingly. "Oh yeah, I've been there," he said.

I thought about Luke all the way home and when I got home, I thought about him more. But I was also thinking about God. It took some time, but I managed to find the Bible my parents had given me for high school graduation—a big, fat study Bible still in its box. I took it out of the box as if it might break at my touch. It still had that new Bible smell.

I opened to the Book of John and I began to read.

And something happened. I don't want to get all Jesus-freaky on you, but there's no denying, that Sunday afternoon, God spoke to me through his Word. I remember reading the words, *God did not send the Son into the world to judge the world, but that the world might be saved through Him*, and I remember wondering, for the first time, *Is this all real? What if this is all real?*

It occurred to me then, that maybe there was more to this God thing than church. More to this God thing than religion even. As I read John's story, I felt like God was telling me that he wanted to know me, and that he wanted me to know him. It suddenly became powerfully personal.

I prayed then, to a God I was really just discovering for the first time. I said something along the lines of "I want to know you. If you're real, and I think that you are, please help me to know you." And I kid you not, I felt a warm and powerful peace fill my body. It was the strangest thing. It seemed to start in my gut and fill my whole body. I didn't understand it, but I somehow just knew that God was there.

Chapter 8
Payday

Weeks and weeks after my first flopped celebration, I got my first Grace Space paycheck. When I eagerly ripped into the envelope, glitter fell out. I'm not even kidding.

I had earned a grand total of 297 dollars. So, not counting my gasoline bill, I was back to zero. I had made enough money to pay off the kickoff kit.

This made me feel better. Part of me still wondered if all of this had been some colossal error, but breaking even allowed me to tell myself, *You've recovered from your initial mistake. Now you can quit at any time and still be ahead.*

I was excited to tell Lisa about this, so I flagged her down outside of the next family meeting, but she interrupted my news to say, "You need to reinvest." Lisa wanted me to spend my first check on Grace Space.

I said, "Of course you want me to buy more Grace Space. You get five percent of my orders!"

She seemed offended. "Darcy! Grace Space is about relationships, not money. I would never put profit ahead of our friendship! I want you to buy more Grace Space for *you*."

"But why?" I innocently asked. "I don't need more Grace Space products."

"Oh but, Darcy," she said, sounding a little sad, "I think you do."

"Why?"

"Well," she paused, as if she were about to deliver some bad news. "You just don't usually look ... well ... *put together.*"

I couldn't help it. I laughed. "Put together? What, am I falling apart?"

"No, Darcy," she said, noticeably *not* laughing. "But you don't look like a Grace Space consultant either. You never wear foundation, so I can see your wrinkles. You're obviously not using the wrinkle cream either."

"Wrinkles?" I said, horrified, "I'm only twenty-four! I don't have any wrinkles yet!"

"Yes you do, Darcy. And you need to do something about them. You also need to start wearing eye shadow, especially the highlighters, and you need to have someone clean up your eyebrows. And while you're there, have them do something about your hair. It's sort of just ... *there*. It's not doing anything for you. I think a good cut could have a really slimming effect."

I was speechless. I couldn't believe how many times I had just been insulted. I didn't know how to respond. I didn't know what a highlighter was, didn't know how to clean my eyebrows, and wasn't sure why I needed a slimming haircut if I wasn't overweight. At least, I didn't *think* I was overweight?

Because I didn't know what else to do, I walked away from my friend and into Priscilla's Grace Space wing. I sat down in a cold folding metal chair and tried to be invisible.

After several minutes of fake prayer and faker sales reports, Priscilla publicly praised me and the recognition had more of an effect on me than it should have. It almost made up for Lisa's little coaching session. She called me up front and proudly said, "We would like to recognize Darcy with an out-of-state award. Darcy booked and completed a celebration in Lowell, Massachusetts! Great job, Darcy! We are all inspired by your success!" The room exploded in purple applause and I returned to my seat, proud as a purple peacock.

Of course, Priscilla didn't mention that I had only sold 125 dollars' worth of product in Lowell, and that I hadn't booked any celebrations from that celebration. But I enjoyed my moment in the spotlight nonetheless.

Soon my good friend Lisa was called up front as well. We were all told that Lisa had "promoted herself" to violet. Priscilla presented her with a new violet suit. The room exploded in purple applause again.

After the meeting, I congratulated Lisa on her promotion. She seemed genuinely excited and this made me genuinely happy for her. I asked her how she did it. She looked at me like I was stupid. "Did you read the literature in your purple folder?"

The English major in me cringed at her use of the word literature as I lied, "Some of it."

"It's all right there in the folder. To get to be a violet, you have to recruit three new Grace Space consultants who have to each sell at least three hundred dollars' worth of product in the same month, and one of those consultants has to have recruited at least one new consultant in that same month. Understand?"

"Absolutely," I said, even though I had no idea what she had just said. All I heard was, "Darcy, you will never be a violet. It's way too complicated."

The next night, I had a party booked with a friend I had made at New Life. Her name was Emma and she lived in a trailer in the middle of the woods in

Clinton. I got there just as her friendly husband was trying to hustle three kids under the age of seven out of the house. As I looked around the cramped trailer for a place to set up my display, I saw him shove the third kid into the cab of his truck.

Emma was still scurrying around, picking up toys and sippy cups. I told her not to worry about it and asked her where to set up. With a magical sweep of her only free arm, she cleaned off the coffee table and pointed to it with her chin.

I smiled and began to go through my setup routine, which by then, I was good at. Emma had obviously worked to make her celebration a success. Six different women showed up, three of whom I recognized from church. Emma opened a family sized bag of no-name-brand Doritos and we all sat down around her kitchen table. The room was so small that our chairs were all touching.

I remember having a great time that night. The women were all sweethearts, and I actually had fun hanging out with them. They seemed genuinely interested in the products, and I had finally learned enough to be able to answer their questions without straining. When it came time to separate them for checkout, there was nowhere for me to go. Emma suggested that I use her bedroom. So, I awkwardly perched on the edge of Emma's bed with each of my new friends, asking each if she wanted to order anything, if she wanted to be a "model" for me, if she was interested in a Grace Space career.

This became especially awkward when it was Emma's turn. There I sat with Emma, on her bed. I suddenly felt like I didn't know her well enough for this level of intimacy. But Emma was excited to order some Grace Space goodies—three hundred dollars' worth. You might think I would have been thrilled, but no. Instead, a sick and sinking feeling of dread filled me. Emma handed me a credit card. I didn't take it. I just looked at her.

There was a long, awful pause. I finally said, "Would you be interested in our payment plan?"

"You have a payment plan?" Emma asked, still holding out her plastic.

"Absolutely," I said, "it's like a reverse layaway plan. You order the products tonight, and you can pay me in installments. But this plan only works with cash or check." Not bad for off the cuff, right?

Emma took the offer. We ordered her the product. She didn't give me any actual money, but promised she would. That night, when I plugged the orders into the Grace Space website, I used *my* credit card to cover it. I didn't have the three hundred dollars either.

Chapter 9
Luke

I was pretty sure I was falling in love with the drummer. Luke just seemed to have such a gentle spirit. He laughed at all my jokes, even the ones that weren't funny. In fact, he had this adorable fake laugh that he used for the not-so-funny jokes. When I said something stupid, he would let out a fake chuckle, and I would feel like a million bucks. He liked me enough *to fake laugh for me*. I wanted to marry him.

But so far, I only saw him on Sundays. We took to sitting together for after-service brunch. I took to waiting for him to ask me out. When he came into the diner one Monday morning, I thought for sure he would.

He was with two men who looked like they were probably coworkers. He introduced me as "his friend Darcy," and he had a twinkle in his eye. When he left, he gave me a hug goodbye, and I realized for the first time that I was a smidge taller than him. I vowed to never wear heels again. (Actually, I had never worn heels, but in that moment, I renewed my commitment to flats.)

Luke was a wiry, muscular man of about five foot eight. I figured (hoped) he was about my age, but it was hard to tell because of his baby face. His unbelievably perfect baby face. I wanted to spend the rest of my life with that face.

That night, I walked into the family meeting, prepared to tell Lisa about my credit card crisis of conscience. We were becoming more like actual friends. We had our disagreements, but I had come to realize that Lisa was a real person just doing her best to make her business a success. She was really just as clueless about this whole thing as I was. (Okay, maybe a little less clueless.)

But when I saw her, I held my tongue. Something was really wrong. It was obvious she had been crying. She wasn't wearing her customary fake eyelashes, and her mascara was streaked. And it took me a second to notice, but she was wearing a lilac suit.

"Lisa, what happened?" I gently asked, sitting down beside her.

She forced a smile. "Oh, I'm fine," she managed to croak out. "I'm just a little overly emotional about having to wear lilac tonight."

"Why did you have to wear lilac?" I asked.

She sighed. "My team didn't meet quota for this month, so I'm back to lilac. Don't worry though, I'll be back to violet in a jiffy." She patted my leg and smiled again, as if I were the one who needed consoling.

"I don't understand," I said, "you have to sell a certain amount every month to stay a violet?"

"Yes," she explained with strained patience. "I have three recruits. Each of those recruits has to sell at least three hundred dollars' worth of product in the month, and one of them has to recruit a new consultant. But don't worry," she assured me again, "I'll just recruit more consultants this month, so there won't be so much pressure on the three I have." She looked at me piercingly and I understood. It was my fault she had been demoted. I felt sick to my stomach. I hadn't recruited anyone. I hadn't even tried, really. I just didn't feel like I *could* recruit someone when I had nothing to show for my own business. How could I say, "Hey, you should come work with me, because I'm making like forty dollars per week and I have to wear a stupid lilac suit! Sound like fun?!"

That was a long family meeting. I sat there like a ton of bricks, not listening to Priscilla prattle on about some nineteen-year-old in New York who had just become the youngest Grace Space Independent

Regional Sales and Marketing Manager in history. Apparently, this was a really big deal. I felt like a really old twenty-four-year-old failure. I was failing miserably at a job I didn't even like. I was sure my life couldn't get any worse.

Then a door opened in the back and a voice said, "Mom, you have an emergency phone call." I responded emotionally to the voice before my brain was able to consciously connect it to a name. So, excited, without knowing why, I craned my neck around along with a hundred other purple-clad necks and looked toward the door. And there he stood. The drummer of my dreams. Luke.

Chapter 10
Out of the Bag

Unlike the other hundred heads in the room, mine snapped back to the front as quickly as it had craned to the back. It was instinctive. It took me a second to realize that the emotion to which my instinct was responding was that of embarrassment. I didn't want Luke to see me in a Grace Space family meeting, even if apparently that meeting was being run by *his mother.*

His mother? My brain was screaming. And crying. How was that even *possible?* I promised myself that if I ever fell in love again, I would make sure to get the guy's last name first.

The next Sunday, Luke acted like he always did, and I surmised he hadn't seen me. But now, allowing him to believe that I was *only* a waitress seemed like a lie. A lie by omission maybe, but still a lie. Though I totally wanted to keep this secret from Luke, I didn't want him to ever *know* I was keeping a secret from him.

In hindsight, I should have just quit Grace Space right then and there. Then I never would have had to come clean with Luke. But of course, I didn't think of that. And of course, I was so poor. And of course, I had so much vested interest. And of course, I didn't want to go back to January recess duty or scraping gum off the bottoms of diner tables. So, after the service, I said, with as much cheeriness as I could muster, "I was surprised to see you Monday night! I had no idea Priscilla was your mom!"

He looked like I had slapped him.

"What?" he said shortly, leaning back in his chair a little, as if trying to create more space between us.

"Oh, I must have forgotten to mention. I dabble in Grace Space, and I was at your mom's house on Monday night. So I saw you when you came in."

He just sat there, for what seemed like a painfully long time. Then he said, "Oh. Sorry, I didn't see you."

"No worries," I said, a little too quickly, and then, because I couldn't think of anything else to say and I was panicking at the thought of the conversation ending, "Do you live with your mom?"

He looked disgusted. "No, of course not. I'm twenty-eight years old. I was there fixing her plumbing, and her phone rang. So I answered it."

I didn't know what was happening between us, but I knew it was bad. And within a few short minutes, Luke got up to throw away his plate without finishing his lemon cake. And then he left.

Driving home, I began to cry. I cried for my life. I was so poor. I was so alone. How had my life come to this? I had done everything I was supposed to do. I was a good girl. I had never gotten into trouble. I had gotten good grades and gotten my degree. I was supposed to have a teaching job and be involved in some furtive faculty romance by now. Yet here I was, waiting tables and trying to peddle lipstick, and wanting Luke, who didn't want me back.

As I parked my car, my phone rang. It was Emma. "Hi! I wanted to talk to you at church but you practically ran out of there. Everything okay?"

"Yep."

"Okay," she said, sounding unsure. "Well, I was wondering if I could talk to you about signing up for Grace Space."

Chapter 11
My First Daughter

I really liked Emma. I considered her a friend. Yet, it never occurred to me to warn her against Grace Space. Instead, I enthusiastically invited her over, saying I would "get her set up pronto."

I don't know that my motives were selfish. I just know I was excited at the idea of bringing a new lilac to a family meeting. I was excited to have some success at this crazy venture. I was excited to have the other lilacs look at me with envy. I was excited to receive Priscilla's public praise.

I did get Emma set up pronto, and when she handed me her credit card for the cost of the kickoff kit, I only paused momentarily. By then I knew that fifty dollars of the cost of a kickoff kit goes straight to the recruiting consultant. In addition, I would receive five percent of all of Emma's sales. And, I would also receive three percent of all her offspring's sales. Yes, Grace Space really did use the word offspring.

Emma had lots of questions. I could answer most of them. When I couldn't answer one, I promised we'd ask at the next family meeting. She seemed sincerely excited about Grace Space, and her excitement was contagious. I became excited too.

I was especially excited at the next family meeting. I walked in with Emma at my side and, stealing only a quick glance at Luke's door, walked straight to Priscilla. I introduced Priscilla as Emma's great-grandmother and Priscilla quickly corrected me. Priscilla was Emma's great-*great*-grandmother.

"Wow, how do you keep it all straight?" Emma asked, wide-eyed.

"Oh, you get used to the lingo," Priscilla said with a smile far brighter than anything she'd ever flashed at me.

In a moment of absolute absurdity, I was jealous over Priscilla's attention, and so, without thinking, I spouted, "I didn't know you were Luke's mom! We go to the same church."

There was that sour candy look again. "Yes, I know. I'm the one who sent you to that church, remember?" And with that, she turned and headed off to greet more new lilacs.

We talked about nail polish that night. For more than an hour. Who knew so much could be said about nail polish? Apparently, Grace Space was rolling out a new line of nail products, so there was a big push to sell the remaining old bottles. We were encouraged to "stock up" as people were very loyal to their favorite colors and would want to buy a whole bunch of the old colors once the new colors were released. Of course, they wouldn't be able to, so we consultants should stock up and then sell the old colors ourselves.

So when I got home that night, I ordered three of each color of Grace Space nail polish.

Chapter 12
Commack

Later that week, I had a celebration in Commack. It occurred to me to give the celebration to Emma, but I didn't think I could spare it. I was having a hard time getting any bookings, and I hadn't done a celebration in over two weeks.

If you've never been to Commack, Maine, you can't imagine how creepy it is. Books have been written about the nineteenth century witches of Commack, Maine. To my knowledge, Commack is no longer the witchcraft capital of Maine, but when my

GPS told me to turn right onto Cobweb Road, I got nervous.

Cobweb Road isn't really a road. It's a narrow gravel path. And it was October 30. And the farther I drove, the narrower it got. And the bumpier. I hit one hole that I was sure was going to break my car in half, and a half mile later, I skirted around a giant boulder, scraping my driver's side window on some low-hanging leafless branches that sounded a lot like desperate fingernails. Despite myself, I let out a little shriek.

I focused on my breathing, and put my faith in the GPS, until the GPS showed I was no longer driving on an actual road. I slowed to a crawl, and started to look for a place to turn the car around and abort the mission when I saw my destination. Thank God.

I got out of the car, looked around for axe murderers, and then dragged my Grace Space suitcase inside. It wasn't exactly a warm welcome. My hostess greeted me, but the rest of the guests stared at me as if I was from some lower caste.

Against my instincts, I began to set up. The nail polishes had come in that morning, so I lined them all up in front of my standard display. The display had grown a little as I had won a few prize products, but it still looked pretty paltry.

I explained to my guests that these were the old colors, and to get them now, because they would be out of stock soon. A woman with orange hair said, "Why will they be out of stock soon?"

I was always grateful when someone engaged in conversation with me, and this time was no different—at first. "Well," I explained, "they are rolling out a new line of colors and a new formula, so they are discontinuing these colors."

"Oh," Miss Orange said. "So, won't the new formula be better?"

I'll admit, I was stumped. "I don't know?" I answered feebly.

"Well, I doubt they would 'roll out' a new formula that was worse than the old one," she said and everybody laughed.

I smiled. She had a point.

I continued the celebration with, "Let's do hand makeovers!" I whipped out the Hand Exfoliator #1, the Hand Exfoliator #2, the Moisturizing Hand Wash, and the Hand Moisturizer. I explained, "This is a great way to give your hands a treat. You start with the Hand Exfoliator #1," and I began to squirt some into each of their hands.

Miss Orange piped up, "Hand Exfoliator #1? How many hand exfoliators are there?" Every word she spoke dripped with sarcasm.

"There are two," I answered without looking at her.

"Why?" she asked.

"Why what?" I said, still avoiding eye contact.

"Why are there two hand exfoliators?"

I did not know the answer to this question, so I didn't answer it. Instead, I began squirting a drop of Moisturizing Hand Wash into each woman's hands and instructing them to go rinse off under warm water. As they lined up at the sink, Miss Orange asked again, louder this time, "Why are there two hand exfoliators?"

I looked at her, and for the first time in a very long time, felt something close to hatred as I said, "I don't know."

"Oh!" she said as if she'd just won a really important contest.

What seemed like many hours later, I found myself one-on-one with Miss Orange in the den.

"Did you have fun tonight?" I asked, doing a great job at civility.

"Did you?" she asked, ignoring my civility.

"Of course!" I lied. "I always enjoy celebrations."

She smirked, indicating that she totally knew I was lying. I didn't care. I was so sick of Commack. "What would you like to order today?" I asked.

"Oh no, I'm not going to order anything. Jaime told us not to order anything, because her cousin Maria is a Grace Space consultant and Maria will give us all her discount."

It took a second for this to sink in. Jaime, the current hostess, had instructed her friends *not to order?* Is this possible? Would somebody actually do that?

"Seriously?" I asked.

"Yep," Miss Orange said, and this time, she actually looked like she sympathized with me. "But tell you what, if you want, I'll book a party and I won't tell my guests not to order. Maybe you'll make a few bucks.

"Okay," I said. "Thanks. Where do you live?"

"Castle Rock," she said. That was like a zillion miles away.

"Castle Rock? What the heck are you doing in Commack?"

"I'm a bellydancer. I had a performance today. Jaime is a bellydancer too. She invited me to this. So here I am."

"Oh!" I said, as if that made perfect sense. "Well, I'm pretty booked up right now, so if you don't mind, I would like to give your celebration to my colleague, Emma."

Chapter 13
Gertrude

After briefly checking my car for witches and black bears, I collapsed into the front seat and headed back out Cobweb Road. I had earned zero dollars that day, but I was happy. I was just grateful to get out of there alive.

When I returned to the land of cellular service, my phone beeped that I had a message. It was difficult to understand the speaker, but I thought she said her name was Gertrude and that she would like to place a Grace Space order.

I almost yelped in excitement. Finally, an order had just fallen into my lap! I was so excited, I couldn't even wait to get home. I pulled into a gas station and called her back.

Her name was indeed Gertrude. She had found my number online, using the handy-dandy "Find a Grace Space Sister" widget. Her voice cracked often, suggesting she was well into her retirement years. She said she hadn't seen a Grace Space catalog in years. Could I come over and give her one? Then she would place her order. I said sure and asked for her address, which she quickly provided. This surprised me. I had noticed most people weren't too keen about telling me where they lived.

I arrived at Gertrude's building, which, incidentally, was just down the street from my parents' house, about forty-five minutes later and took the elevator to the second floor. She answered approximately one half second after I knocked.

A short, wide woman opened the door. Gertrude was leaning on a walker, but she only looked to be in her forties. She invited me in.

I had to pause to consider how I would go about such a thing as entering her apartment. I put one foot inside but then I wondered what to do next. There was stuff stacked from floor to ceiling on all sides. I watched Gertrude walk ahead of me and marveled that the stacks weren't caving in on her. Her walker rubbed on either side, but the stacks stood firm. Leaving a cushion between us, I followed her into her apartment.

About twenty feet in, the path we were on took a sharp turn to the left. As I turned, a cat jumped from one stack to another, its paws nearly brushing against my bangs as I went, and I couldn't help but let out a little yelp of terror.

Without turning around, Gertrude said, "Oh don't mind Sunshine. She's always flitting about. Looking for a mouse I suppose."

I couldn't imagine how any creature could find a mouse in this apartment, but I just kept placing one foot in front of the other, until finally, we reached a chair. It was a recliner, but there was so much stuff behind it, I doubted it did much reclining. A few feet in front of the recliner stood a television. There was no TV stand though, just a stack of stuff propping it up.

You may be wondering what all the "stuff" was, but I couldn't really tell you. Though I ended up in that apartment several times, I still can't be specific. It was just ... stuff. Papers. Boxes and boxes. Cardboard boxes, plastic totes, milk crates. There were books, and yarn, and boxes of food. An empty bird cage.

Gertrude said, "Have a seat."

I looked around. There was only the one recliner.

I looked at her, obviously confused.

She pointed at the one recliner.

Because I didn't know what else to do, I sat. As soon as I did, I was alarmed to find my left shoulder only mere inches from a tower of pizza boxes. I hoped they were empty.

She said, "Did you bring me a catalog?" Of course, I had. I handed it to her. She put on some tiny reading glasses, and leaning on her walker, began to flip through the catalog.

And she flipped.

And she flipped.

She studied the catalog. Silently. While I sat there. I didn't know what to do. I had never been so uncomfortable in my whole life. And she flipped. Finally, thank the heavens, she finished the catalog. Then, much to my horror, she went back to the front and began again.

Sunshine, at least I thought it was a cat, some blur of fur, leapt over my head and landed on the pizza box tower, causing it to lean perilously close to its tipping point before it rocked back to its former uprightness.

As I sat there trying to form an escape plan, she said, "They used to have this perfume I liked, but I can't find it."

"What was it called?" I asked.

"I don't remember," she said, not looking up from the catalog.

"Well, all of our perfumes are excellent, if you'd like to try something new."

She looked up. "Do you have some samples?"

I hesitated. "Uh, yes, but not with me."

"Could you bring some over later?" she asked.

I really didn't know what to say. Not only was it already nine o'clock, but how hard should I have to work to make a perfume sale? Still, the perfumes were forty dollars, which would mean twelve dollars in my pocket. "Uh … sure. When I get a chance, I'll drop some off."

She grunted. No really, she actually grunted.

A few more minutes passed and then she said, "I've got a catalog here somewhere. Sit tight," and with that, she disappeared into a sea of stuff. I could not see her, but as I looked into the abyss, I saw another cat scratching its back on the bird cage. This distracted me until she returned, clutching a faded Grace Space catalog in her hand. She flipped it open to the right page on the first try and pointed at a perfume. It was called "Hadassah."

A few months prior to that, I wouldn't have gotten the reference, but I'd been spending a lot of time in the Bible lately, so I became superbly annoyed that Grace Space had named a perfume after Queen Esther. It just seemed disrespectful to me, but at that point, anything would have annoyed me.

"Uh, I don't think we have that perfume anymore," I said, flipping to the front cover, where it said that this catalog was from 1993. *How could she possibly have located this so fast in this sea of stuff?*

She then said, "That's okay, I still have some."

"You know what?" I began. "How about you spend some time with the catalog, and when I come back with the perfume samples, we can talk about what you might like to order." I said this, of course, having absolutely no intention of ever coming back. I was lying through my teeth, but I had to get out of there. It was getting hard to breathe, and I didn't want to lose control of myself and say something really mean to this woman.

"Oh no, stay awhile," she said. "I'll make you some tea."

I was scared of her tea, so I made up something about having to get home to let the dogs out, and I worked my way toward the door.

And then I was out, gasping for air in the hallway. And then I was outside, gasping for more air. And then I was in my car, my breathing slowly returning to normal. I decided then and there that I was done. I was done with Grace Space. This was ridiculous. I wasn't making any money. I didn't like the company. I had lost Luke's friendship. And I had just nearly been crushed to death by the leaning tower of pizza boxes. It was over. I was sure of it.

As I pulled into my parents' driveway, I saw Steven come out of his house. As I got out of the car, I saw him cross the road. *Now what?* I grimaced.

Steven was holding a Grace Space order form. I didn't have any idea how he had gotten his hands on one, but I didn't care, because Steven had filled out the order form for 421 dollars' worth of stuff. I looked at him, nearly crying with gratitude. He smiled. "Got all my Christmas shopping done with one whack," he said.

Chapter 14
Priscilla's True Colors

The next Sunday, I decided to skip brunch and was on my way to my car when Luke caught up to me. "Darcy!" he said, touching my elbow.

Now, you should know I was furious with him for refusing to be my friend just because of Grace Space, but when he touched my elbow, even though it was through a shirt, all was forgiven. I looked at him, wide-eyed and ready to say "I do."

"Yes?" I said instead.

"I owe you an apology."

You're darn right you do! I thought.

"For what?" I said.

"Look, it's really complicated. But I just really hate Grace Space. I hate everything that company stands for. I hate everything it's done to our family." He paused. It looked like he was trying to decide whether or not to continue. "I like you," he said, "so I don't mean to be rude. I just don't want anything to do with the color purple." He smiled. Then he turned and walked away, leaving me speechless beside my car.

The next night, Emma and I carpooled to the family meeting. It was a closed meeting, and I was dreading it. Those always took longer. When we walked in, the place was solemn. A few lilacs were crying. I wondered who had died. For just a brief insane moment, I worried about Luke. Then I realized that no one here would care if Luke died. Well, no one except me. And maybe his mother.

"What is going on?" Emma whispered.

"I don't know," I whispered back. We instinctively moved toward the back of the room and sat down in two ice cold folding metal chairs, where we would remain for the next two hours.

Within minutes, Priscilla took the stage. (The stage was just a small platform up front, but Priscilla treated it like a stage.) "Welcome, family," she began. "I assume you've all heard the news. Today is a sad, sad day for Grace Space, but ..." she paused to dab at her eyes with a tissue, "we are strong and we will carry on, by the grace of God."

I stared blankly at Emma, who stared blankly back at me. We seemed to be the only two people in the room who didn't know what was happening.

"It is important," Priscilla continued, "that we do not dwell on the specifics of the event. Instead, we need to figure out how we are going to respond to the reactions of our customers. We will assure them that the woman in San Diego is not representative of us or of our company. We do not need to defend or explain her or her actions. We do, however, need to defend Grace Space. We will do this by focusing on all the positive things our company does." There was some paltry applause at this, but Priscilla waved it off. "We also have another distressing point to discuss, and this one hits a little closer to home." Priscilla paused and looked directly at me, her eyes burning with contempt. "It has come to my attention that some Grace Space consultants have tried to use illegal financing with their customers." She was still looking at me, but it didn't occur to me that she was talking *about* me until she said, "There is no such thing as a reverse layaway plan. The Grace Space Independent Sales Consultant Handbook clearly states that all orders must be paid in full before they are placed."

I could feel my cheeks burning. I couldn't look at Emma. I didn't know whom she had told, and I was sure she hadn't meant to get me in trouble, but I was still embarrassed to look at her. I didn't want her thinking that I had created reverse layaway just for her. It sounded too much like charity.

The meeting continued with talk about new hair clips and some prayer, but I couldn't listen. I just sat there, staring straight ahead, waiting for it to be over.

When it was over, I abruptly walked away from Emma and cornered Priscilla. "Do you have a second?" I asked.

"What?" she said.

I assumed she hadn't heard me over the purple din, so I said again, "Do you have a second?"

"What?" she said again.

I couldn't believe it. I leaned toward her and said, obnoxiously loud, "Do you have a second?!"

She stood up straight and said, "Well, you've used it."

My blood was boiling. *Did this woman have any idea how to communicate like a human being? How had she ever come to be in leadership?* I said, "I don't appreciate being reprimanded in public. I did not do anything 'illegal.' That is an outright lie. All I did was lend Emma some money—"

Priscilla interrupted me. "It is against the rules to lend money to a consultant underneath you. That is a way to inflate your leadership score."

I did not know what a leadership score was, but I didn't care. I said, "She wasn't a consultant when I lent her the money. She was just a customer. And she doesn't have any money! Don't you ever feel guilty taking a credit card from someone who obviously can't afford our products?"

Priscilla grabbed my arm and yanked me into another room. I was momentarily distracted (and delighted) by framed pictures of Luke on the walls. Young Luke in a football uniform. Young Luke smiling in a cap and gown. An older Luke smiling in a different cap and gown. *I didn't know Luke went to college*, I thought, but then Priscilla snapped me back to the argument at hand. "Do *not* challenge me in front of my women!" she practically hollered, so close to my face I could feel the moisture of her breathe. "You are planting negative seeds, you ungrateful brat!"

I stood aghast. No one had *ever* spoken to me like that. I took a deep breath. "I quit. Priscilla, I quit. And I'm going to tell everyone what this company is really like. I'm going to tell anyone who will listen that you are not only cruel, but quite possibly insane. Even your own son hates this company." And with that I stomped away from her, slamming the door in her face.

When I got to the car, Emma was leaning on it. "I'm so sorry," she began.

"Don't worry about it," I interrupted her. "I just quit Grace Space. I really don't care, but I do wish you the best. Come on, let's go home. I'm exhausted."

After a few minutes of riding in a comfortable silence, I asked, "Did you find out what the woman in San Diego did?"

Emma started to laugh. "Yes. She hung a Grace Space bag on a customer's doorknob, and the bag was

…" Emma sucked in some air and then laughed some more.

"The bag was what?" I asked.

Her cackle leapt out of control. "It was full of …" She tipped her head back and gasped for air.

"Emma, what the …"

"It was full of poop!" And she let out a shriek of laughter. Tears were rolling down her face. And it was contagious. My tired brain couldn't even process the story. A Grace Space bag full of poop? *What did that have to do with us?* I too started to laugh. It was just so absurd. But, the harder I laughed, the harder I laughed, and soon, I had to pull over and get control of myself. Both us of laughed ourselves to the point of exhaustion and then sat there, recovering.

"Was it human?" I asked.

Emma looked at me for a second and then burst into laughter again. I was befuddled. "Was what human?" she shrieked, rocking back and forth in her seat.

"The poop!" Then I was at it again, laughing so hard my obliques started to hurt.

Emma took an exaggerated breath, so that she could spit out an exasperated "How the heck should I know if the poop was human? I don't think so! Why would someone poop in a bag?"

I looked at her incredulously. "That's your argument?" I asked. "Because it makes perfect sense to fill a Grace Space bag with another species' poop?"

All told, we must have sat there for fifteen minutes, laughing like a couple of fifth grade boys who just can't get enough poop jokes. When we had laughed ourselves dry, I finally drove us home. As I pulled up next to her car in the Park-n-Ride, Emma turned serious. "Please don't leave me Darcy."

"Huh?"

"Please don't quit Grace Space. I need you. I really need the income and I just don't think I can do this without you." She sat still, staring at me, her hand on the open car door, as if she was waiting for me to promise Grace Space forever. I couldn't do it.

"I'll think about it," I said.

"Good enough," she said. And she was off.

Chapter 15
Gertrude Again

When someone banged on my parents' door at two a.m., I briefly hoped it would be Luke. Of course, that was a ridiculous hope. It had more likelihood of being the Loch Ness Monster.

It wasn't Luke. Or Nessie.

It was Gertrude.

I panicked. Though I had thought of it often, I hadn't gotten around to getting up the courage to actually drop off the promised perfume samples. Now here she was, on my parents' front steps. In the middle of the night.

I considered my options. She banged on the door, "Darcy! Are you in there?"

Trying desperately to gather my composure, I opened the door.

"Gertrude! It's two o'clock in the morning! What are you doing here?" *And how do you know where I live?*

"You never brought me my samples!" Gertrude snapped.

"Do you want them right now?" I asked.

"That's why I'm here," she said.

"Hang on," I said, and shut the door in her face. I rummaged around and came up with two samples. I opened the door and handed them over.

"There are only two?" she said accusingly.

"Yes, that's all I have," I said. "This is my parents' house! You have to go!"

"Seriously? You still live with your parents?" she said with abundant disgust.

I slammed the door in her face. Hoping it was all just a nightmare, I crawled back into bed. Of course, I couldn't fall asleep, wondering if my mother had heard the mayhem. I tossed and turned and thrashed around for what felt like hours. The last time I glanced at the clock, it said read quarter past four. *Ah well*, I thought, *I don't have the breakfast shift tomorrow, so I can sleep in.*

Priscilla called me at seven.

"I need to apologize," she said.

"Okay," I said groggily.

"Are you still in bed?" she asked accusingly.

"Yes," I said groggily.

"You should be up by now. The early bird gets the worm, you know!"

"Okay," I said groggily.

"Listen, Darcy, I don't want you to quit Grace Space. So, as an incentive for you to continue with your hard work, I would like to offer you a celebration tonight. I was going to do it, but you can have it. It's in Portland."

"I have to work tonight. Sorry," I said, even though I wasn't.

Priscilla paused. I enjoyed imagining how hard she was having to work to be nice to me. "That's okay," she continued. "I also have one on Friday night. That one's in Belfast," she said.

"Wow, you sure do get around," I said, no euphemism intended.

"Excuse me?" Sour candy again.

"Nothing," I said. "Sure I'll take your Belfast celebration."

"Great," she said, and she gave me the address. I tried, but I couldn't fall back asleep. I couldn't quite figure out how I had managed to quit Grace Space and still not be done with it.

I vowed that after Friday's party, I would quit, for real.

That night, I went into work with a skip in my step. I felt oddly free, like a weight had been lifted. I was in such a good mood that I didn't even get upset when a table full of teenagers left me a handful of pennies and pocket fuzz for a tip.

That night, I was let go from my waitressing job. It wasn't my fault, I was assured, they were just downsizing the staff as they neared the slower winter months.

I couldn't help it—I burst into tears.

On Friday, I drove to Priscilla's celebration in Belfast. I had to use my credit card to fuel up in order to get there at all. On the way there, I seriously evaluated my life. I decided I needed to find a job—any job—in a school. None of this current foolishness was doing anything to further my teaching career. And I really did want to be a teacher. I had the student loan debt to prove it.

Then I got to 217 White Street. I found myself in the historic district, surrounded by stately mansions. I instinctively straightened my skirt and spit out my gum. *Unbelievable*, I thought.

That night, I made seven hundred dollars in profit and recruited an eighteen-year-old named Jacelyn. I also booked two more celebrations, one of which I gave to her.

Driving home, I was in such a good mood that I was even nice to Gertrude when she called to tell me she would like to place an order. I was in such a good mood that I even agreed to stop by and collect her order, and payment, on my way home.

When I knocked on Gertrude's door, I heard her yell, "Come in!" I tried to do so, but it was a lot scarier navigating that apartment in the dark without her in the lead. At some point, I must have made a wrong turn, because I was suddenly looking at her on the toilet.

Her bathroom door was stuck in the open position, as boxes were stacked against it. "Oh, sorry," I stammered, and turned to quickly go in the other direction. In doing so, I almost stepped on a cat I did not recognize. The cat squealed in protest and Gertrude called, "Thunder, are you okay?" from behind me.

I found the living room and waited for Gertrude to join me, which she did shortly. "It's nice to see you, dear," she said. "How are you?"

"I'm great, thank you. You said you wanted to place an order?"

"Ah yes, I did like one of those samples, but I had to give all my money to the drugstore, you know, for my prescriptions and the like, so I don't have enough money this month. Do you think you could give me a few more samples?"

I stared at her.

She must have sensed I was about to blow, because she then said some magic words, "Also, I was looking in the catalog, and it said that I could become a Grace Space consultant. Do you think I could actually make some money at it?"

I did *not* think she could make some money at it, but she would be recruit number three. With three recruits working under me, I had a shot at a violet suit. I still didn't understand the ins and outs of it, but I knew that much. And suddenly, *I wanted that violet suit.*

It doesn't make any sense now, but in that moment, I had a rush of adrenalin, and I told Gertrude that absolutely, she could make a mighty fine Grace Space Consultant.

Chapter 16
A Violet Is Born

Of course, Gertrude didn't drive, so Emma and I picked her up on Monday night. Of course, Gertrude didn't come down to street level on her own, so I had to go up to her apartment and get her. Of course, she invited me in, but I refused, citing that we would be late if we didn't get going.

Gertrude put on a multicolored rain hat, a bright pink slicker, and yellow rubber rain boots that looked about three sizes too big. It wasn't raining. "You look great. Let's go," I said.

I had to help her and her walker into the car, but I didn't even care. I was on my way to a family meeting with a car full of recruits! I was on top of the world. Jacelyn the rich kid from Belfast met us there, and I didn't even sit with Lisa that night. I sat with *my* team. It was an open meeting, so we focused on the models and Priscilla talked about how to take "working vacations" that can be tax write-offs.

At the end of the meeting, I handed Gertrude a welcome pack and a consultant contract. "I've filled this out for you," I said. "I just need you to sign here."

"What is it?" Gertrude asked.

"Oh, it's just your sign-up sheet. Just fill this out, and order your kickoff kit and you'll be on your way to a new career!" I knew I sounded too much like Priscilla in that moment, but I couldn't help it.

"How much is the kickoff kit?" Gertrude asked.

This detail wasn't included in the catalog pitch, and I mentally kicked myself for not mentioning this to her beforehand. The cost of this kit might really interfere with Gertrude's Grace Space plans. "Three hundred dollars," I said.

But Gertrude took it in stride. "Okay," she said, "give me a few weeks to get the money together and then I'll give you this paper back."

"Sounds great," I said.

As we backed out of Priscilla's driveway, I saw Luke pulling in. He waved. I waved back. I had skipped church the day before because I didn't want to face him. In fact, I hadn't consciously admitted it to myself, but I was really trying not to have feelings for him anymore. But seeing him there, flashing me that perfect wave and that perfect smile, I really, really missed him.

I managed to get myself home and into the shower. As soon as I stepped into the tub, my phone rang. It was Gertrude. I let it go to voicemail. A few minutes later, my phone rang again. Sure it was Gertrude, I stomped over to look. It wasn't her. It was Jacelyn. I answered. Jacelyn had a zillion questions. I tried to answer them, and we ended up talking for more than an hour.

She called me again the next day, and the next day, and by Saturday, she had completed three celebrations and recruited two new consultants. I was both jealous of her success and grateful that she was *my* offspring. The big, fat checks would be rolling in any day.

That Sunday in church, I couldn't take my eyes off Luke. I tried to think about God, I tried to focus on worship, but he was just such a good drummer! All that banging and pounding was very distracting. At the after-service brunch, I slid into the seat across from him and said, "Okay, tell me the truth. What's your issue with Grace Space?"

I said it with more boldness than I felt, but he smiled and that made me feel braver. "We don't want to get into that right now, Darcy."

I shuddered at hearing him say my name and got braver still, "So when do we want to get into that?"

He smiled again and looked away. I'd like to think he blushed, and maybe he really did. Then he looked right at me, his blazing blue eyes digging into mine, and said, "Darcy, we really can't have this conversation. I'm sorry." And he got up and walked away.

I felt like I had to choose between the possibility of Luke (it certainly wasn't a sure thing) and my only source of income. I resented him for making me make that choice. And I just wasn't ready to give up. I had to prove to Priscilla that I could be as successful as she was. I had to prove my parents wrong. I had to prove all the critics wrong. I had so much proving to do!

Before the holidays, sales did pick up, but not as much as Priscilla had promised. I had a few phone orders and a few online orders and a few Christmas celebrations, but I still hadn't caught up on bills since losing the waitressing income. Jacelyn, on the other hand, was on fire. That girl could sell! At family meetings, I could almost feel the envy of the other lilacs as they heard about Jacelyn's sales figures. Then in early December, I also managed to convince my aunt to join Grace Space. My mom was mortified.

So I didn't invite her to my promotion meeting. It was my big night. I was finally a Grace Space Independent Team Leader. I expected to be excited. I expected to feel like I had accomplished something. But as Priscilla formally presented me with my violet suit, I didn't really feel any of that. Even after all the applause, I still felt like something was missing. Then, on my way out of the meeting, Priscilla handed me a bill for the violet suit, and what measly sense of accomplishment I had left fled.

"What's wrong?" Emma asked on the way home.

"Oh, nothing," I brushed her off. She looked at me suspiciously, and I felt guilty for giving off negative energy. She was working really hard at her Grace Space career, and she needed me to be positive. I tried to steer my mood back toward glass half-full.

When I got home, Gertrude was sitting in my parents' living room. My glass was instantly bone-dry.

My mom gave me a wry smile and left the room.

"You forgot me!" Gertrude snapped.

"What?" I asked, exhausted.

"You forgot to pick me up!" she said, louder.

I had taken Gertrude to the last four family meetings. She still wasn't a consultant, and I had finally figured out that she had no intention of ever becoming a consultant. She just wanted to be recruited. She just wanted to be wanted.

"Enough, Gertrude! I can't take this anymore!" I snapped back.

She looked like I had slapped her. But she didn't look mad, just stunned. "You've got a case of anxiousness," she said. "Come here, honey, let me massage your scalp."

What?

"You want to give me a scalp massage?" I asked, alarmed, and marveling at how odd the words sounded in my own voice.

"Yes, it will relax your anxiousness. I can do it. I'm trained. Come on in and lie down."

"Um … no thank you," I said. "You need to go now, Gertrude."

I waited for her to get up. But she didn't budge.

"Please, Gertrude. I'm sorry I forgot you. But you have to leave. This is still my parents' house. You need to go … please." I was begging, and she knew it. Finally, she got up and shuffled toward the door. I opened it for her. She stopped in the doorway and looked at me. She didn't say anything. She just stared. "Good night," I said, and she finally walked through the open door. As I shut the door, I saw my mother watching from the top of the stairs. I couldn't tell what she was thinking. I was sure I didn't want to know.

Chapter 17
Nutter Butters

Priscilla instructed me to donate my lilac suits (she foolishly assumed I had ever bought more than one) to Goodwill. I couldn't imagine who on earth would want such a thing. And if someone didn't recognize it as a Grace Space costume, they would certainly figure it out when they saw the Grace Space logo embroidered on the chest.

There were some perks to the violet suit. It was slightly less ugly and ill-fitting than the lilac suit was. Slightly. Violets were also gifted with more free product, so that Christmas, I gave Grace Space to everyone. They pretended not to be annoyed, and I really didn't care if they were.

My heart wasn't really in Christmas. I was pining for Luke and angry that I was single for the Lord's birthday. Christmas morning at my parents' house with my two siblings and their spouses felt like torture. My mom got me a stand mixer, which I thought was a really strange gift for a woman with no kitchen. I wondered if she was trying to tell me something. As I was analyzing the meaning behind the Kitchen Aid, my sister-in-law handed me a package wrapped in what looked like Easter wrapping paper. There was no tag.

Gingerly, I peeled away the pastel eggs to reveal *The Collected Love Poems of Pablo Neruda* and a bag of pistachios. Neruda is my favorite poet and pistachios are my favorite nut.

"Who is this from?" I asked.

Everyone in the room ignored me, busy with their own Christmas cheer.

"Who is this from?" I repeated, louder and snarkier.

They all stared at me. "I don't know, honey," Mom said. "What does the tag say?"

Wow, I never would have thought of that. "There is no tag, Mom."

"Oh, well then, how would I know?" And then they all went back to their Christmas cheer.

Steven. It had to have been! And I was both touched and freaked out. *How did Steven know me so well? And how did he sneak a present under my parents' tree?*

No one else seemed to care about my mystery, so I stomped to my room just like I had when I was fourteen and misunderstood. Only a little worried that Steven would be inside my bedroom wrapped in a bow, I crossed the threshold and shut the door behind me, so that I could marathon *Jericho* in peace.

The next morning, I was climbing into my car to go buy some marked-down Christmas candy, when I saw Steven standing in his doorway. He looked like he was waiting for me to say something, so I sort of half-shouted across the street, "Thank you, Steven. That was very kind of you."

He looked confused. "What was kind?"

I stared at him for a moment, confused. *Was he just messing with me?* "The gift. The poetry. And the nuts. Wasn't it from you?"

"Well, that depends," he said. "Did you like it?"

I laughed awkwardly because I didn't know what else to do. Then I climbed into my car. Then I sat there. Thinking. *The gift was from him, right? I mean, who else could it be from? He was just messing with me, right?* And so I climbed back out of the car, crossed the street, and for the first time in my life, I knocked on Steven's door.

"Yes?" he said, his face alight with joy.

"For real, that gift was from you, right?"

"For real, no it wasn't."

"Steven, don't mess with me. You didn't leave that package?"

"No, I did not. Here, I got you these," he said and handed me a poorly wrapped package of Nutter Butters.

"Uh … thanks," I said.

"You're welcome," Steven said. "You do like Nutter Butters, right?"

"Ah, yes, Steven, absolutely, thanks." *At least these were wrapped in seasonally-appropriate paper.*

And I walked away, wondering if I should have consumed those mystery nuts after all. *But they had gone so well with* Jericho. I presumed that, had the pistachios been laced with rat poison, I would already be dead. I would probably be okay.

My sales completely tanked after Christmas. Even Jacelyn's figures slowed down. I missed a car payment and couldn't contribute to the house heating bill. Things weren't looking good.

That Sunday at church, the pastor talked about how the cold weather caused financial hardships for people, and if any of us were struggling, that we should let him know, because the church could help keep people safe, warm, and fed. I caught Luke looking at me. I wondered if Luke knew I was broke, and if so, how?

At the next family meeting, Priscilla started talking about nationals. She was talking so excitedly, her voice was practically squeaking. And women all around me appeared to be just as excited as she was. I learned that, every March, all the Grace Space consultants in the universe descend on Cleveland for the annual national conference.

Priscilla said, "It's so inspiring! It will change your life! There are so many people there just like you—it's like the world's biggest family meeting! And all of these rich, successful Grace Space women give you pep talks! It's so inspiring!"

Well, I could use some inspiration. But not at that price tag. I learned that every year, the gals all rent a super awesome charter bus and load it to the gills. It costs fifty dollars to ride the charter bus, two hundred dollars to stay in the conference's host hotel (with three other women, so that's sharing a bed with someone), and another two hundred just to attend the conference.

There was just no way I could come up with 450 dollars. And when Priscilla put her hand out to collect my registration form, I told her as much. "You have to go," she responded, not looking at me, but collecting forms from others around me. "It's non-negotiable." And she continued on. I wondered how she planned to physically force me onto a charter bus.

Then I learned that Luke would be driving.

Chapter 18
Ejected

On Sunday, I didn't even wait till brunch. I marched right up front, stood in front of the drum kit, folded my arms across my chest, and said, "So, you can't talk about Grace Space, but you'll drive the bus?"

Luke smirked at me and my knees almost gave out. Literally. I almost fell down right there in front of God and everyone. People would've thought I'd been touched by the Spirit. "Who told you?" he asked.

"Lisa," I said.

"Lisa who?" he asked.

"Lisa Provost, my Grace Space mother." I said the last part with some irony, trying to get him to laugh. Of course, he did.

"I don't know her," he said.

"Of course you don't, you want nothing to do with Grace Space. Right?"

"Darcy, my mom asked me to drive. She's paying me. I could use the cash. I'm sorry if this makes me a hypocrite."

"I didn't call you a hypocrite, Luke. I would never say such a thing. I just don't know why you won't tell me what you've got against my company."

"*Your* company?" he asked, one luscious eyebrow raised. He stood up then, and looked me in the eyes. "If you can't figure out what's wrong with Grace Space, then you won't understand if I tell you."

I decided then to be angry at Luke. I didn't care how godly, how handsome, how sweet he was. I decided I was mad. Better than mad, I was *indignant*. I stomped to my row and threw myself into the pew. Emma came in and sat beside me, but I could hardly even utter a greeting. Then she leaned over and said, "Will you sleep with me at nationals? I really don't want to sleep with anyone else."

And that, my friends, was funny. I laughed. My mood brightened as it always did when I was around Emma, and I relaxed. But I was still mad at Luke.

The next night proved to be the most entertaining family meeting I ever attended. A lilac named Lori came to the meeting *hammered*. The people seated near her apparently knew of her condition and tried to cover for her, but it wasn't easy. She was loud, and she kept saying, "I'm not drunk" far louder than any sober person would ever say it.

People kept shushing her, and she was quiet for a few moments and then she loudly (and oddly proudly) announced that she had to go "take a leak." She tripped over a folding chair on her way to the bathroom and fell flat on her face. No one laughed, except for her, who was apparently unscathed, because she rolled around howling with laughter, not pain. She got up, tears rolling down her cheeks, and came face to face with Priscilla. Now if that doesn't sober you up, nothing will. Lori stopped laughing. She put on her best I-haven't-been-drinking face and said at a normal volume, "Excuse me, Priscilla, I was just trying to get to the restroom." At this, people *did* laugh, and as Lori tried to skirt around her Grace Space Independent Regional Sales and Marketing Manager, Priscilla grabbed her by the arm and yanked her toward the door. Priscilla was hissing at her the whole way, but I couldn't make out what she was saying. Then she promptly threw her outside, sans purse or jacket.

I waited for someone to defend her, and no one did. Without thinking, I stood up and headed for her stuff. As I reached for her purse, Priscilla snapped, "Leave it!" She said it as if she was talking to a dog. So, like any untrained pooch (my parents' Labs had taught me well), I ignored her command and grabbed Lori's purse and coat and headed for the door.

Priscilla physically blocked my way. Two other violets headed toward the door too, and I wondered if there was actually going to be a physical altercation. Is there such thing as a Grace Space brawl? "And just where do you think you're going?" Priscilla asked.

"I'm going to take my Grace Space sister her coat so she doesn't freeze to death, and then I'm going to drive her home so she doesn't wrap herself around a tree." I reached for the doorknob, and Priscilla actually slapped my hand.

"She made her bed. Let her lie in it," Priscilla hissed. "Our behavior has consequences."

I reached for the doorknob again, and said, "Or I could show this woman the mercy God has shown me and get her home safely. And if you touch me again, I'm report you for assault."

I ripped the door open so forcefully it was like I was expecting it not to open and I went out into the cold. Priscilla hollered at me, "If you leave here now, don't come back! You are officially kicked out of my family!"

Without turning around, I said, "That's totally against Grace Space rules." Lori, who was leaning on her car, chuckled at that and it occurred to me that her car keys were probably in her purse. Turns out, so was her flask. I drove her home in her car, figuring I could call Emma when I got there and have her come pick me up after the meeting. But I didn't need to do that.

Luke pulled in right behind me.

I walked Lori to her door and then I walked back to his truck. "Hi?" I said.

"Hey," he smiled, "thought you might need a ride back to your car, and maybe even a body guard."

"How did you know?" I asked.

"Ah, Mom's walls are thin. I was watching basketball with my dad. We heard the whole thing." He smiled again. My heart melted, again. So maybe I wasn't mad at him. Then he said, so softly I almost couldn't hear him, "I'm impressed, by the way."

I couldn't think of anything to say, so I stayed silent, but it was a comfortable, easy silence all the way back to my car. I thanked him. He said, "You're welcome," and then he went back inside. I sat in my car waiting for Emma to come out. And I couldn't stop smiling.

Chapter 19
Emma Spills the Beans

I had been kicked out of Priscilla's family. I figured the best revenge I could get would be to marry her son.

I never found out if I was actually kicked out, or if Priscilla could even do such a thing, but I did stop going to her meetings. This did not affect my income and I wondered why I ever went to those things in the first place.

I know you're wondering, so yes, I'll admit: Priscilla's attempt to fire me did give me an easy out from Grace Space. I could have just quit right then and there. But it was almost time for nationals, and I wondered if maybe it was only my unit that was this nutty. Maybe, when I got to nationals, I would see that Grace Space wasn't such a bad company after all. Maybe I could work my way up the ranks and have my own family, whom I would be really nice too. Maybe we could actually *be* a ministry to women. I'm sure my husband Luke wouldn't mind building me a Grace Space wing on our home, right?

And really, now I wanted to succeed just to tick Priscilla off.

So I made it my mission to raise the funds to get to nationals. I began to offer people celebrations wherever I went. When the woman at the drive thru handed me my fries, I handed her a lipstick sample stapled to a business card. When a man at the drive thru handed me my fries, I handed him a sample for his wife. I put baskets in local stores, with a sign that said "Weekly Drawings for Winners!" Then I called everyone who filled out the card and offered them a celebration.

I called one woman who called me something I cannot repeat here. I asked her why she had filled out the card. She claimed she hadn't. I called one woman who turned out to be an eight-year-old girl who had filled out the card. I called more than a hundred women, and five of them agreed to do a celebration. At one of these hard-won events, a baby vomited carrots all over my only violet suit.

Another of these hard-won events was supposed to happen in Augusta, our state's proud capital. When I got to the address, I double-checked the card she had filled out, just to be sure. I was fairly certain that no one could live in this building. It looked like it was going to fall in. The whole building was listing to one side.

With no small trepidation, I entered through the front door and was instantly overwhelmed with a horrible smell that I thought might be urine. I climbed the stairs, looking for apartment 3b. Graffiti was spray-painted on every wall. There was trash all over the floor. There were cobwebs in every corner. The closest one was full of flies, making me wonder what had ever happened to the spider. A pair of panties hung from an exit sign. When I reached 3b, I raised my hand to knock on the door and I heard what I swear sounded like rattling chains. I lowered my hand. I should have knocked. I willed myself to knock. But I didn't. I backed away slowly, and then I turned around and ran. I ran to my car and never looked back. I never called to explain myself, and that woman never called to ask why I hadn't shown up. It wasn't my proudest moment, but I very much feared dying that night, or worse.

I had nightmares all night after that, so I decided to take the next day off. But then the dogs went berserk with their daily letter carrier alarm.

I got up to get the mail and was dismayed to find that several orders had arrived. Unlike some companies that ship products directly to the people who wanted them, Grace Space ships to consultants, so the consultants have to make deliveries. This, I was told, "fosters relationship building." It never fostered much relationship building for me, because I almost always just repackaged the products and mailed them to their rightful owners. I didn't have time to drive all over tarnation making deliveries, especially when most of my celebrations were happening at least an hour from my house. Whoever had this brilliant personal-deliveries-fosters-personal-relationships idea was obviously not operating in rural Maine.

Still, when I saw the single pair of earrings that had been ordered by Briana, who lived three streets over, I recognized the foolishness of putting it back in the mail. I decided it would be good to get out of the house. I broke the lilac-suit-rule though and left the house to deliver the earrings in jeans and a sweatshirt.

My incognito attire did nothing for me. As I approached Briana's home, I saw her through the window. Then I heard her holler, presumably to children, "Get in the kitchen! The Grace Space lady is here!" Hoping that I had heard her wrong, I rang the doorbell. I heard her dog bark, but there was no human response. I gave it a good two minutes, and then I hung her earrings on her doorknob and returned to my car, walking back past her minivan, which was of course, parked in her driveway.

Despite all this, I did manage to eke out a small income during the month of February. I also consumed nothing but Ramen and water the entire month, so it's a wonder I didn't contract scurvy.

So, at church a few weeks before nationals, when I met Luke in the hall as I was practically running to the free brunch, and he asked me if I still planned to go to Cleveland, I said, "Of course!"

"You realize my mother's not going to let you on the bus?"

I stopped running and turned to look at him. "Seriously?"

"Yeah. She won't let you on, but I can get you on if you want."

I laughed, taking a step toward him. "You're going to sneak me onto your mother's bus?"

"If you want," he said grinning.

"Hmm, so you're going to help me advance my Grace Space career, even though you are adamantly opposed to Grace Space?"

His grin faded. "I offered you my help. You can take it or leave it." He walked past me, down the hall toward the food.

I called out, "I'll take it!"

And he responded "okay" without turning or slowing down.

When I got my food, I couldn't see Luke anywhere, so I sat down with Emma.

"Why so glum?" Emma asked.

I sighed. "I'm just wondering why Luke is so anti-Grace Space."

"Oh, good grief, you would be too if you were him."

"Huh?" I asked.

Emma looked at me. "You mean you don't know?"

"You mean you *do* know? And you haven't told me? Spill it!"

Emma leaned over toward me, "You realize this is gossiping, right?"

"Just tell me!" I snapped.

"Okay, well, according to the grapevine, Priscilla used to be a nice person. She used to be all like mother-of-the-year and super involved in church. Everybody loved her. Then Grace Space turned her into a monster. Luke met his fiancée—"

"His *what*?" I interrupted.

"His fiancée," Emma repeated, "do you want to hear this or not?"

I nodded eagerly.

"Okay, so he met his fiancée at Bible college. She moved to Waterville to be close to him. As soon as she moved, Priscilla recruited her, of course. But Amy—that was her name, I think—Amy was really good at Grace Space, like really good, better than Priscilla. Priscilla wasn't a Manager yet, back then, she was just a consultant, and some of her clients started dealing with Amy because they liked her better. So, of course, Priscilla decided to torture Amy. I don't know the details, but Priscilla did her best to get rid of Amy. And Amy left town. She's still a bigwig Grace Space

114

Manager somewhere in Massachusetts. She's part of the reason that Priscilla is successful, but Amy left Luke. And Luke blames Grace Space."

I'm pretty sure my mouth was hanging open. Poor Luke! I analyzed this story all the way home. *What kind of a girl would choose Grace Space over Luke? She must have been crazy!*

Shortly after I got home, Dominique called. I still hadn't met her. She lived in Portland, so she ran her own family meetings, but Priscilla had recruited her in the first place, so she was still my grandmother, technically.

"Hi, Darcy, I was wondering if you could do me a favor," she began. "We are coming to the end of our business month, and I'm only a hundred dollars short of maintaining the leadership score I need to stay at my current bonus level. I was hoping you might place an order for me? Do you need any personal products?"

I was confused on so many levels. Yet Dominique seemed to have cast some sort of spell on me.

"Okay," I said. And I went online and used my MasterCard to order some personal products, wondering if any of them would "clean up my brows."

Chapter 20
Blizzard

One Friday night I had a celebration scheduled in Weld. That's about a fifty-mile drive. I had a good feeling about the celebration. I had met Kirsten at another celebration and she had ordered a ton. She seemed very excited about Grace Space and had been enthusiastic about her own celebration. In other words, this was shaping up to be the celebration that Grace Space recruiters presented as normal, but I had yet to experience.

The trouble was, when I turned on the television that morning, the cute weatherman told me not to leave the house. "Winter Storm Watch" was emblazoned across the screen all day, and my phone kept beeping weather warnings at me.

I honestly didn't know what to do. I had grown up in Maine. I knew how to drive in snow, but I also knew that it was slightly insane to drive to Weld in a blizzard.

Lisa made the decision for me. "You can't cancel," she said.

"Yeah, but …"

"You can't," she repeated. "You'll be fine. You've got all-wheel drive."

"Won't people think I'm crazy?"

"No, they'll think you're reliable."

"But what about the safety of Kirsten's guests? Don't I have some responsibility to them?"

"They are grown women," Lisa said. "They can make their own decisions. All you have to do is get there. Leave early and drive slow, and you'll be fine." She sounded like she was tired of discussing it. I was tired of thinking about it.

Foolishly listening to Lisa and desperately needing the money and the leads this celebration could potentially generate, I got into my tired old car three hours before the celebration was supposed to start.

The roads were *horrible*. I considered turning around at least a dozen times, but greed, or stubbornness, or just plain stupidity pushed me onward. I made it past Wilton, but then it seemed as if the plow trucks just stopped.

Driving through three inches of fresh snow at about twenty miles per hour, I realized that I had made a very, very bad decision. I decided to find a place to turn around. I would call Kirsten and reschedule. It suddenly seemed like such an easy thing to do. But I couldn't find a place to turn around, and while looking for one, I hit something that felt like a bump in the road and lost control of my car.

As I yanked the wheel to my left, the car continued to the right, toward the forest. I said a quick prayer, mostly apologizing for my own idiocy, as my car skidded to a halt among the trees.

Completely stopped, I caught my breath and noticed, with immense gratitude, that I had landed between two trees, with only inches to spare on either side. The trees were so close, I couldn't open either car door. My hands visibly shaking, I fumbled for my cell phone, but of course, I had no signal. I was in Perkins Plantation in a blizzard. Of course I had no signal.

A significant panic set in. I could all too clearly picture myself freezing to death in the name of Grace Space. Thanking God that my parents had at least raised me smart enough to wear winter boots, if not smart enough to stay home in a blizzard, I climbed into the back of my car and pushed a door open through the snow. I stepped out into the snow, which was deep enough so that some spilled into my boots.

Renewing my hatred for the Grace Space skirts-and-pantyhose-rule, I trudged my way through the snow, desperately clutching my cell phone. I got back to the road and prayed again for a miracle. And I began to walk. And I walked. And I walked some more. And nary a bar appeared on my phone.

Eventually, just when I was certain I would lose my ears and toes to frostbite, I saw a house. Thank you, Jesus. Without pausing to consider that the house might be filled with snowbound cannibals, I knocked on the door.

The house was not filled with snowbound cannibals, but with an elderly angel couple who leapt into action. Within minutes, I was sitting next to a woodstove, sipping on a cup of hot cocoa and dialing my father's phone number.

Of course the sweet old woman asked me why I was out in such a storm. And though I wanted to lie, I figured I should suffer the embarrassment. So I told her the truth. And she nodded understandingly. "My daughter got caught up in Grace Space when she was about your age. It happens to the best of us." And then she patted my hand.

Then her husband told me hunting stories until my father showed up, about an hour later, with his four-wheel drive and tow straps. Dad aptly pulled my car out of the woods, and then followed me all the way home. To date, he has never said a word about the incident.

Chapter 21
The Secret to "Selling" Lots of Cold Cream

I did reschedule Kirsten's celebration, and on my way to Weld, I stopped at my angel friends' house and dropped off some maple syrup. (When people are nice to you in Maine, you give them maple syrup.)

The celebration went as fabulously as I dreamed it would, so I drove home in a great mood, but my mood was crushed with unbelievable efficiency when I entered my parents' house.

The first thing I noticed was the smell. It was as if someone had forced cold cream into my nostrils. The next thing I noticed was Max, my parents' eldest Labrador, licking what looked like cold cream off the kitchen floor.

Despite the ample evidence, it took me a minute to piece together what had happened. To the right of Max's nose was an overturned tub of cold cream. Just to the right of that was the cover of said tub, chewed into three pieces. One of the pieces was stuck to the cardboard box that my most recent delivery had come in. The box was in shreds, so the piece I was looking at proudly declared "ace spa" in bright purple letters. This was no day at the spa.

As I stared, Max finished licking up the cold cream and lay down on the floor, whipping his tail back and forth, sweeping bronzing powder across the linoleum as he went. Stan came trotting into the kitchen then, holding a crushed tube of sunscreen in his teeth, the remains of something bright red smeared all over his teeth. The third Lab, Smokey, was nowhere to be seen. I followed a trail of eye shadows and mint foot lotions into the living room, where Smokey lay in a big pile of body glitter, contentedly munching on some pomegranate-scented sugar scrub.

I turned on the light to better survey the damage and was astounded to find lip gloss on the lamp shade. *How was that even possible?*

I sat down and I wept. I didn't even want to think about how much this was going to cost me. I didn't even want to think about having to clean this up before my parents got home. I couldn't even think about how much damage that much Grace Space could do to a dog's digestive tract. I couldn't process any of it. I just sat there and wept.

Eventually, I did peel myself off the chair and get to work. And eventually I did sit down at the computer and reorder all of those products. And no dogs were harmed in the making of this catastrophe.

When I won an award for sales that week, I didn't tell any of my Grace Space sisters how I had sold so much cold cream in one week.

Chapter 22
Desperate Measures

One happy, insignificant Wednesday, I got a "Violet Suspension Warning Letter," stating that none of my recruits had recruited anyone new this month, and so I was in danger of being demoted to lilac. I had one week to "inspire my offspring to reproduce." Yes, it really said that.

I hadn't heard from Jacelyn in weeks. She wasn't returning any of my calls or texts. I didn't want to harass her, so I had stopped calling. My training told me to alert Priscilla, but I wouldn't do that to anyone.

I figured that Jacelyn knew where I was and how to find me. If she needed me, she would call.

My aunt would probably have been willing to help, but if I called her, I knew it would get back to my mother, and my mother would be disgusted that I was pressuring my aunt to recruit. My mother would have a point.

That left Emma.

I called her up. "Hey, listen to this," I said, and I read her the letter.

"Does that mean I have to recruit someone?" she asked.

"Well, you don't have to, but I sure wish you would, yeah. I just don't want to go to nationals as a lilac. Then Priscilla will think that I've failed because she stopped helping me."

"So wear the stupid violet suit to nationals. Who is going to know?" Emma asked.

"Priscilla will know. She knows everything."

"Does she know you're in love with her son?"

"I'm not!" I snapped, wondering how Emma knew. *Was it that obvious?*

"Okay, but what's she going to do, rip your suit off and then wrestle you into a lilac one?"

"Please, Emma," I pleaded. "I need your help."

"I know, Darcy, but I'm just so *tired*. I've tried to recruit everyone I know. Not only are people not interested, but they are *mean*. I'm tired of people being mean to me. In fact, I think I'm going to quit celebrations altogether. I've got a few clients who order pretty regularly. It gives me a steady stream of a little money. That's enough for me."

This is one of the worst things a gracie can hear. Priscilla had warned us against language like this: the sound of a lilac losing steam, cooling off—"the beginning of the end," Priscilla had called it.

Then I had an idea. Emma had never received one of those fifty dollar bonus checks one gets with a new recruit. Those could prove to be quite the incentive. "What if we could get Gertrude to sign on under you?"

Emma snorted. "Gertrude? You're not serious."

"I am serious. I'll do all the work. You get the credit, and the cash bonus. And I get to go to nationals in violet."

"Yeah, but then don't I have to deal with being Gertrude's *mother* for the rest of my life?"

"Aw, come on, she's not so bad. Just don't ever go to her apartment … and don't let her into yours. And don't let her massage your scalp."

"What?!" Emma asked, understandably alarmed.

"Nothing," I said, "Do we have a deal?"

Emma sighed. "Whatever."

"Emma, I love you!" I shrieked and hung up the phone. I called Gertrude.

Of course, I had to go over there. Of course, Gertrude had no money. So I broke the rules again and offered to float her. She still didn't bite. She looked at me skeptically.

"What is it, Gertrude? Don't you want to be a Grace Space consultant?"

"Yes … well, sort of," she said.

"Well then, what's the problem?" I asked.

"Um, if I sign up, then I'll be like a zebra that turns into a donkey."

What in tarnation? "I'm not sure I follow you?" I asked.

"Well, right now you're my friend because you want me to join your club. But once I join, you won't be my friend anymore. I've seen it happen."

I wasn't sure if she'd seen it happen with Grace Space or with zebras, but I said, "Gertrude, I promise, I will still like you. I will still be your friend. Nothing between us will change."

Her face lit up in a brilliant smile.

"As long as you promise not to call or visit me in the middle of the night," I added. She looked confused. "Never mind," I said. "Just sign here."

And Gertrude happily signed.

Two days later, Gertrude called me at five o'clock in the morning. "Great news!" she said, "I just got my tax return! Now I can go to nationals!"

Chapter 23
Bad News

I opened my door a few hours later to find Gertrude standing outside it with a tape measure.

"Good morning?" I said.

I also noticed Steven peering at us through his kitchen window. I waved to him cordially. He mistook this for an invitation. Soon he was headed my way, his coffee cup in hand.

"Good morning," Gertrude said.

"How can I help you?" I asked, wishing I had some coffee of my own.

"I just need you to measure my bust," Gertrude said.

"Your what?" I asked.

"My bust! I'm trying to fill out this form here," she said, waving the lilac suit order form in my face, "and I don't know what size I need."

I grabbed the form out of her frantic hand. "Well, I'm pretty sure I don't have to measure your bust. These suits come in standard sizes. What size dress do you usually wear?" I asked.

"I don't know," she snapped. "My mother buys all my clothes."

Steven let out a barking laugh from behind her, but Gertrude didn't seem to notice. I gave him a dirty look. To Gertrude, I said, "So, maybe we could call your mother and ask?"

"Can't. She's dead."

I was honestly stumped.

Steven wasn't. "Maybe you could just check her tag right now, Darcy, and see what size she's wearing." If looks could kill, he would have been one hurting unit that moment, but his idea was valid. I asked Gertrude to turn around and then I ever so gently flipped over the top seam of her shirt.

The tag had been removed. "Uh-oh," I said, "no tag."

"Try her skirt," Steven smirked.

I sighed. With a trembling left hand, I carefully lifted her shirt, and with a trembling right hand, I gently folded over her waistband. There was a tag, but it was so faded, I could not read it. "Twenty!" I announced.

"Twenty?" Gertrude said doubtfully.

"Yep," I said, maybe even a little too helpfully, pointing to the size twenty option on her form. "Just circle that and you'll be all set."

"Okay," she said, and spinning expertly on one leg of her walker, she headed down the walkway.

I looked at Steven. "Not a word," I said. He obliged, and headed back across the street.

The next Sunday, Luke ushered me into the church library. I pretended not to be thrilled. The church library had never felt so romantic.

"What's the plan?" he asked.

"What's what plan?" I asked back.

"How do you plan to get on the bus?" he asked.

"I thought you were going to get me on the bus," I said.

"Well, I will. I'll be at the bus by seven to get it warmed up, but we don't leave till eight. You can get there early, and get on the bus. I can put you in the baggage compartment, or you can just hide in the back of the bus. But, if we're going to do that, we'll need a few women in on it. Otherwise, someone is bound to give it away that you're on the bus."

"You are seriously considering shoving me into the baggage compartment?" I asked, incredulous.

"What?" he flashed those perfect teeth at me. "It would be perfectly safe unless we get in an accident."

I playfully punched him in the shoulder and instantly regretted it. *What am I, twelve?*

"So then, it's decided," he concluded. "We'll need someone who is in on it."

"Okay," I said, "I'll ask Emma."

As we left the library, I was relieved no one saw us. That could have looked far less innocent than it was, the two of us sneaking out of a dark library. Granted, we *were* conspiring against my future mother-in-law, but it still wasn't what it looked like.

I hurried to the sanctuary and slid into Emma's pew. I started to tell her the plan, including her role in it, when she interrupted me. "Darcy, I've got some news," she said. I couldn't imagine what was more important than my stowaway plans, but I paused in the name of friendship. "Last night, Dan asked me to resign from Grace Space. It's not bringing in the money that I told him it would, and he thinks it is taking too much time away from him and the kids. He says it's just not worth it. I'm sorry, Darcy, I really am."

I was floored. And I'm not proud of this, but I said, "Do you think maybe Dan could wait till after nationals?"

Emma looked as if she was expecting me to say that. "Sorry, Darcy, I sent my resignation email last night."

My flesh was very angry in that moment, but thank God for giving me the thought: *Do not act like Priscilla.* So I forced a smile, told Emma I understood and still loved her, and I calmly walked away. It was a good thing I hadn't taken the lilac suit to Goodwill after all.

Before I got far, Emma reached out and stopped me, "Darcy, I appreciate you taking this so well, but there's something else you should know."

"What?" I asked, finding it hard to imagine what else she could say.

"Before I resigned, they told me that all of the money you earned from my sales? Well, they're going to deduct it from your future checks. I'm so sorry, Darcy." Well I hadn't seen *that* in the fine print. I nodded, trying to calculate how much money that would be.

Luke was still lurking by the front pews, talking about March Madness, so I walked in that direction. When he saw me, he looked concerned, so I knew I wasn't hiding my anguish as well as I had hoped. He walked away from his buds, and toward me. My heartrate increased. "What is it?" he asked.

"Emma's not going to be able to help," I said.

"Oh, is that all?" he said, sounding relieved.

And for reasons that I will never, ever understand, I chose that moment to say, "Luke I know what Grace Space has done to your life, and I just wanted to say that I am so sorry." His face softened. He nodded at me slowly, his eyes never leaving mine. We stood there in the middle of the aisle in the front of the sanctuary, staring at each other for what seemed like a blissfully long time. Then he nodded again, squeezed my arm, and turned and walked to his drums.

Chapter 24
Recruit Number Three, Take Two

The bus was scheduled to leave on Wednesday morning. I was considering not getting on it. I wasn't sure I wanted to go without Emma. It might sound silly, but I was concerned about having to sleep with someone else. I knew that someone would have to sleep with Gertrude. That frightened me.

I also didn't want to go to nationals in lilac. I just couldn't handle that level of failure. I went to bed Monday night borderline depressed. It took me a long time to fall asleep, and then, just when I was about to nod off, I had the idea of a lifetime. I sat bolt upright in bed and looked at the clock. It was two a.m. It would be a long wait till dawn, when I could reasonably make a trip across the street.

By the time my alarm sounded at seven, I had fallen back asleep but my Skillet ring tone brought me back to life in a jiffy. I bounded out of bed, brushed my teeth, and threw on some sweats. Oh, how Priscilla would disapprove of me working like this. I bolted across the street and rapped on Steven's door. As expected, he answered within five seconds.

"Yes?" he said with obvious delight.

"Steven! I need a favor!"

"Sure, what's up?"

I hesitated for just a second, aware of the lunacy of what I was about to say. "I need you to become a Grace Space consultant, just for a few days," I said.

He let out a short bark of a laugh. "What?"

"Look, it's a really long story, but I need you to become a consultant, right now, so that I can wear violet to Cleveland. Then, when I get back, you can quit."

"A-huh," he said, as if I was actually making sense. "But don't I have to be a woman to be a makeup lady?"

"No, I checked. The law forbids such discrimination. In fact, there are several male Grace Space consultants."

"Okay, sure, come on in." I hesitated, partly because I'd never been in his house and partly because

I was shocked he had just agreed to my plan. "What?" he asked. "You worried I'm a serial killer?"

"No, of course not," I said, and entered his home. He took the form from my hand and offered me a seat. He sat down and began to fill out the form. I looked around. The house looked remarkably, well, *normal*. The walls were covered in photographs. I was relieved to see that none of them were of me.

"Three hundred dollars?" he asked, shocked.

"Don't worry, I'll pay for that," I said, having no idea how I would pay for that. "And I'll take all the products off your hands, unless you want them. I can use them for celebrations."

"Celebrations, huh?" Steven paused, looking at me. "You've changed, you know?"

"How so?" I asked, annoyed. I figured that Steven didn't know me well enough to know whether I had changed.

"You're always more stressed out now. You're always tense. You don't laugh as much." So there I had it—I had been psychologically profiled by my stalker. Perfect. As he handed me the form, he asked, "Do I have to buy a lilac skirt suit?"

I couldn't help but laugh. "No," I said.

"Well then, what will I wear to nationals?"

Chapter 25
Stowaway

Gertrude, Steven (dressed as a civilian), and I met Luke at the bus at seven o'clock sharp. It took Steven six trips to get all of Gertrude's bags on the bus. Gertrude couldn't move the bags herself, because of the walker. I tried to help, but those bags were *heavy*. I could not imagine what Gertrude had packed for a four-day trip to Cleveland. The three of us settled in the back of the bus and waited.

When we saw lilac women approaching, I slouched down in my seat and Steven buried me in Gertrude's luggage. He sat in the seat beside the luggage, and Gertrude sat in front of me. I expected them to have to explain the baggage in the cabin, or the presence of a man in the cabin, but all the women avoided Steven and Gertrude as if they were contagious. I had built a pretty mighty dream team there, hadn't I?

Only Priscilla mentioned us, and did so from the front of the bus. She motioned toward Steven and said, "Everyone welcome Steven, Darcy's latest recruit." She said my name like it caused her physical pain to do so. Some turned to wave at Steven. Most ignored him. And we were off. I stayed slouched for as long as I could stand it, even managed to nod off for a while, but when I awoke, I desperately needed to go to the bathroom.

I needn't have worried. We were in the back of the bus, and all the women were busy playing on their phones and tablets. I was able to slide to the restroom and back without being noticed.

When I returned to my seat, Gertrude whispered to me, "Is Grace Space a cult?"

"I don't think so," I said. "I think a cult, by definition, has to have a charismatic leader."

"Oh," she said thoughtfully. "I just was thinking that because we were all the same, you know, they try to make us all act the same and look the same and think the same—"

"Yeah, I know," I interrupted her, scared someone would hear her and start a bus riot.

When we stopped in Rochester, New York, Gertrude brought me a burger and fries. She asked me if she could have my pickles. I obliged.

It wasn't until Pennsylvania that I caught Priscilla staring at me coldly. Someone had ratted me out. But she didn't say a word, let alone throw me out of the bus in the middle of I-90. We continued to Cleveland in peace and we arrived at the Cleveland Marriot without incident.

Chapter 26
Nationals

I volunteered to room with Steven and Gertrude, obviously. We got away without another roommate, because no one wanted to sleep with Steven.

I was so excited that I ironed my violet suit and didn't even complain when Steven demanded that we watch *Three's Company*.

Sleeping with Gertrude wasn't so bad. Turns out she was quite considerate, though she snored louder than a chainsaw sans muffler. I didn't get much sleep. But that was okay. I was in Cleveland and I was about to see the real Grace Space, a Grace Space not run by Priscilla.

The next morning, the dream team headed to the continental breakfast. I was amused to see Gertrude put at least four individually-wrapped bran muffins in her purse, but then I was alarmed to see her also drop in a boiled egg.

Keeping my distance from Gert and Gert's purse, I led my team to the monstrous conference room. And the place was *packed*. I had never seen so much purple.

Steven looked quite out of place, not because he was a man so much as the fact that he was wearing khakis. The violet suit who registered us looked at him suspiciously over her spectacles. "I just signed up," he explained. "Haven't ordered my suit yet." It was all coming a little too naturally to him.

We got our packets and started looking for empty seats, and I muttered to Steven, "Do they really make lilac men's suits?"

"I have no idea," he said.

We found three seats together near the front. As far as we could tell, we were nowhere near anyone else from our Maine "family." But then, abruptly, Lori sat down beside Steven. She leaned over to me. "I never got to thank you," she said, "for getting me home that night." She flashed me a big, sincere smile. It occurred to me that her smile was the most authentic thing in the room.

"No prob," I said. I probably should have thanked her back. I might have helped her get home

144

safely, but she had saved me from countless family meetings.

When Eve Alexander took the stage, the room erupted in applause. Eve was a Grace Space founding mother, and she launched the national conference with a prayer that she read off cue cards.

"Father in heaven," she began, "we ask for your blessing here today. We ask for your blessing over these brave women over the next few days. We know how you love the color purple, Father, and we pray that you will shower us with wealth. We thank you again, Father. Amen."

I was *so* glad Luke wasn't there for that. At least, I assumed he wasn't. I had no idea where he was. But I knew he would be disgusted by that prayer. I was pretty disgusted myself.

What followed Eve's prayer was what Grace Space called "testimonies." I expected these to include statements of faith, but they did not. One after another, purple suits from all over the country took the stage and told their story. Each one of them went something like this:

> When Grace Space found me, I was desperate. I had nowhere else to turn, no way to support myself. But Grace Space saved me. My mother and grandmother showed me the way. I worked hard, and today I am rich. I have given my kids a better life because I have lived the Grace Space way.

Seriously, the "testimonies" were so similar there is no way they weren't at least partially scripted. By the fourth purple speech, I had had enough, but a glance at the program told me we were nowhere near done. I began to panic. *What had I done? Where was I? Who was I? What was I doing in* Cleveland *in the middle of this insanity?* I suddenly felt smothered by the ubiquitous purple.

Purple drapes on the walls, purple balloons tied to the chairs, purple confetti on the floor, purple eye shadow, purple eye*lashes* ... I couldn't breathe, I was having my life's first bona fide panic attack. I sat there, sweating, trying to slow my breathing, when Steven leaned over and whispered, "I am so scared right now."

And that, my friends, was the funniest thing I had ever heard. I laughed, and I laughed hard and loud and long. Within seconds, everyone within fifty feet was staring at me, but I just couldn't stop. Of course Steven caught my laughter and joined me. We were disrespecting Grace Space, a serious offense, I realized, but I just couldn't care. All I could do was laugh.

Then a woman in front of me turned around and, using several expletives and an incredibly sinister tone, told us to shut up. It worked. I stopped laughing. I wept instead. I wept because I was part of a company that let a woman as mean as the one in front of me join up. I wept for all the stupid things I had done that had brought me to that point.

146

Suddenly, I had a question in my head, and I couldn't bear one more moment of not knowing the answer. Still crying, I got up and left that room in the middle of another testimony. I didn't tell Steven or Gertrude where I was going, but they followed me, such loyal sidekicks that they were. Lori was only a few steps behind them. They all caught me at the elevator.

"Where are you going?" Lori asked. "Are you okay?"

For the first time in a long time, I didn't have to force a smile at that question. "Yes, Lori I'm fine. I just had to get out of there. I'm quitting Grace Space."

"Oh!" she said as if that made perfect sense, and then she sidled into the elevator with the rest of us.

We got off at the eighth floor, and Gertrude asked, with no small trepidation, "Are we leaving?"

"I don't know yet," I said. "I just need to check something in the room. You guys can go back if you want. You don't have to go with me."

"Yeah, right," Steven said, and the others seemed to concur.

After three tries, my key card worked and I was in the room, ripping my laptop out of its bag.

"What are you looking for?" Steven asked.

"I need to know how much money I've made in Grace Space," I answered.

"You need to know that right now?"

"Yes, shh … I have to concentrate." I opened my ledger spreadsheets and began totaling. And I learned that, since August, I had earned a net total of $971.23. I sat back, appalled, and stared at the screen.

"Why are we all standing here looking like we just solved a mystery?" Lori asked, reasonably.

"I'm sorry, Lori. I don't want to be a bad influence, you know, negative seeds and all," I said. "But I thought I was making money. I mean, I sold a lot of stuff, and a lot of money went through my hands. I cashed a lot of small checks. And Priscilla and the others *told me* I was making money. I even got prizes for sales, but I didn't actually make any money."

"Don't be so hard on yourself," Steven began. "A thousand bucks is a thousand bucks."

"Not really," I said. "That's a thousand bucks spread over six months. I mean, if I was looking at a real job, I'd be bringing in less than two thousand dollars per year. That's not a yearly income! No one can live off that!"

"But wait," Lori said. "How does Priscilla make so much money?"

"I have no idea," I said, "but I wouldn't be surprised if her income is exaggerated. Think about it. She tells us she is rich. This motivates us to work harder, which makes her closer to rich. It's like she can lie her way to wealth."

I could tell they were all with me, and I wasted one second feeling guilty, till I realized that this guilt too, was part of the brainwashing. Of course they don't want us expressing negativity, or reason—it makes it so much harder to pull the wool over our eyes.

"Well, now what are we going to do?" Steven asked.

"I have no idea," I said. "We're in Cleveland for two more days. Do you think Cleveland has a zoo?"

Gertrude sprang to life at this. "Zoo!" She clapped like a child. Then she returned her hands to her walker and held onto it as she hopped up and down. My heart filled with a newfound love for Gertrude. She was one odd duck, but she was growing on me.

There was a sharp knock on the door. I instantly knew who it was. Steven opened the door to a particularly sour-faced Priscilla. She pushed past him and into the room, staring directly at me as if the others weren't there. "You want to tell me what you're up to?"

"We're just taking a break," I started but then thought better of it. I didn't have to be scared of her anymore. "Actually, I'm quitting Grace Space. I think Steven is too. I'm not sure what the other two's plans are."

Gertrude then shouted, "Priscilla, you are a bully! I don't want to work for you! I quit too! You are nothing but a meanieface!"

Steven laughed. "Yeah, what she said."

Lori looked from Priscilla to me, and then back to Priscilla, shrugged and then said, "See you guys later," and left, presumably to return to the conference room.

"If you guys are no longer representing Grace Space, then you need to vacate this property," Priscilla said.

"Um, what? Last time I checked, you didn't own this hotel. And we paid for this room."

"Yes, you did, but you paid the Grace Space conference rate, and I'm going to report you to the hotel staff, and they're going to kick you out of here."

"Nice try," Steven interjected. "You might control everything in Waterville, Maine, but your control is pretty limited here. I'm certain that at the sight of my credit card, they will let us stay in this room. Now get out, before *I* call the hotel staff."

Priscilla hesitated long enough for me to ask her, "Priscilla, does it bother you how poorly this company represents God?"

She looked confounded. "What's that supposed to mean?"

"I mean," I explained, sounding gentler than I felt, "that this company is named after grace, but we don't really present grace to the world. We present greed and dishonesty and then we say we're doing it in God's name. Don't you think there's something wrong with that?"

"Yippee!" Gertrude interjected nonsensically. I think she was cheering me on, but none of us appeared sure.

Priscilla spoke through tight lips, and it looked like she was reciting something, "I think that we work hard, and God blesses those who work hard, and people who fail at Grace Space will say anything to try to stop those who succeed." And with that she turned and left the room. I hoped I'd ruffled her feathers on a level that mattered.

We waited a while to see if someone would come from the front desk to kick us out, but of course no one did. We decided, after a short deliberation, to go to the zoo. Steven paid our transportation costs and admission, of course, because Gertrude and I were broke.

Steven took hundreds of pictures of hundreds of animals. He even caught an image of two giraffes touching tongues. I was so sure that would go viral. I tried to focus on the animals, but all I could think about was Luke. I so wanted to share my news with him.

Chapter 27
The Happy Ending I Promised You

Turns out Steven had spent some time in Cleveland and knew his way around. We also learned that Steven had been pretty much everywhere. His photography chops had taken him all over the world.

Steven treated us to dinner by the river. Gertrude enjoyed the tiny winding river so much that the next day, Steven took us on a river cruise. At one point, Steven got seasick, and Gertrude offered him a scalp massage. He gladly accepted, and I tried not to stare. Even though I was completely consumed with thoughts of Luke, I was also honestly enjoying my two new friends.

I didn't see Luke until Saturday morning, when it was time to load up the bus. I wanted to run up and give him a big hug, but he was busy heaving purple luggage into the belly of the bus. As I got on the bus, I caught him looking at me, but I couldn't tell what he was thinking.

He caught hold of me on my way out of a service station near Buffalo. He grabbed my elbow and gently pulled me to the side of the path. Then he kissed me. With his lips. On my lips. I was completely unprepared. Before I even knew it was happening, it was over.

He pulled back and looked at me. "Wait," I said, "can we try that again? I can do better." He laughed. "I quit Grace Space."

"I heard," he said, and he kissed me again. And it was better than the best kiss I'd ever had. I'm pretty sure it was the best kiss that has ever happened, to anyone, ever, anywhere on earth.

On our way back to the bus, I said, "I'm sorry. About everything. I'm really embarrassed that I fell for all of it. Can we just pretend this never happened?"

He laughed, but he didn't answer me.

When I got back on the bus, Steven looked like someone had kicked him in the stomach. *Oh no*, I thought. *He saw us.* I sat down, unsure of what to say. Of course he had seen. He was the most observant man in the universe.

"You love him?" he asked, without looking at me.

"Yeah, I think I do," I said, as gently as possible.

"And he loves you?" he asked.

"I don't know," I whispered.

"He does," Steven nodded. Then he asked, "Is he the one who gave you Neruda and nuts?"

I was confused. "What do you mean? I thought you left me that present."

"I told you I didn't," Steven said, sounding a little exasperated.

"I know, but I still thought you did. I thought you just wanted to be anonymous."

"Why would I want to be anonymous? I would have—"

Gertrude interrupted him, "Are you talking about Christmas? That was me! And I wasn't anonymous! I wrote a note on the inside of the wrapping paper!" *Oh, of course!* "In fact, I was really hurt that you never thanked me."

I turned to look at her, beyond surprised. "Gertrude, how did you know me well enough to get me Neruda and pistachios?"

"I looked at your Facebook page," she said matter-of-factly. "My neighbor has a fancy computer."

Steven began to laugh. I joined him. Oh, of course. Facebook. Kind of makes stalking obsolete, doesn't it?

We got home late Saturday night. I stood around waiting for Luke to finish helping everyone with bags.

When he had, he walked me to my car. "I guess I should ask you out on an official date," he said.

"Then I guess maybe I should say yes," I answered coyly. He gave me a quick peck and then opened the car door for me. "There's one thing you should know though."

"What's that?" he asked.

"I don't think your mother's going to like me."

More Books by Robin Merrill

Shelter

Daniel

Introducing Gertrude, Gumshoe

Gertrude, Gumshoe: Murder at Goodwill

The Witches of Commack, Maine

The Jesus Diet: How the Holy Spirit Coached
Me to a 50-Pound Weight Loss

More Jesus Diet: More of God, Less of Me,
Literally

Printed in Great Britain
by Amazon